Alpha Barman

SUE BROWN

PROLOGUE

JT pushed the white envelope containing his resignation across the polished expanse of the desk. “I can’t stay here, Lukas.” He was doing his level best to hold onto the remnants of his control in front of his section leader but, if JT didn’t get the hell out of Lukas’s office, he knew it wasn’t going to last.

Lukas Romaine ignored the envelope. A man in his late thirties who’d once been beautiful enough to stride down a Paris catwalk, he was worn by years of herding cats, as he described his operatives. He gazed sadly at JT. “You don’t have to leave. Not yet. Don’t make a hasty decision you’ll regret later.”

“Yeah, I do. I can’t stay, Lukas. Not now. Not after what he did.” JT had known he’d have a battle on his hands to get Lukas to accept his resignation, but he was tired and he’d hoped Lukas would accept it without question. After three years as part of his team, he should have known better. Lukas questioned everything. As a senior section leader in a covert ops organization it was his job to question everything, usually to death. JT had been happy, working for a private organization which specialized in extraction, human and otherwise, from ‘difficult’ situations.

“Riley’s locked up. He can’t get anywhere near you,” Lukas said. “You’re safe now.”

“It doesn’t change anything, Lukas.” Nothing would change what Riley Ward had done to JT’s life.

Lukas leaned forward in his seat, his knuckles whitened

as he gripped the arms of the chair. “JT, I promise you he’s going to pay for what he did to you.”

JT’s patience snapped. “Do you think locking Riley up is going to ‘make him pay’ for killing my sister?”

“He can’t hurt you.”

“He already *has*. Riley was my best friend since grade school and he killed his wife—*my* little sister. Do you know how that feels? I’ve lost them both.” JT resisted the urge to wrap his arms around himself as he remembered bursting into his sister’s kitchen to see her lying blood-soaked on the floor with Riley standing over her, a knife in his hand. As he’d watched, a drop of blood had fallen to the floor, adding to the crimson puddle next to her.

“I’m sorry, JT.” Lukas exhaled sharply. “I know how much you loved them. Riley was one of *us*, too. But he’s gone. And now I’m losing you?”

“I’m sorry, too.”

“No, you’re not.” Lukas sighed as he picked up the envelope. “Are you sure about this, JT? If I process this there’s no going back. You’re finished here.”

“Accept my resignation, Lukas. It’s better for all of us this way.”

“What about Mitch?” Lukas asked.

JT stiffened. “What about him?”

“You’re really going to walk away from your boyfriend?”

“You knew?”

Fuck! He and Mitch had been so careful to keep it quiet because inter-office romances were strictly against the rules. They’d been together for over two years and never a look or a kiss had passed between them during ‘office hours’.

Lukas slammed his hands on the desk, half-rising in his fury. “Don’t treat me like I’m stupid. You’re in my section. I knew from the first fuck.”

JT stood and mirrored Lukas' stance as he put his hands on the desk and glared at him. "Don't take it out on Mitch. It was my fault."

"I'm pretty sure you broke the rules together," Lukas said drily, his anger fading as quickly as it had flared. "But you haven't answered my question. You're leaving the section *and* him? Is that what you want?"

JT looked away, unwilling to let Lukas see his inner turmoil. "It's for the best."

"You're a fucking idiot if you think that, JT." Lukas sounded tired. JT had to ignore the hurt in his voice. It was the only way he'd get through this.

"Maybe, but I can't stay here. Everyone treats me differently and everything reminds me of Sharon and Riley." JT was sick of his team tiptoeing around him as if they expected him to fall apart. He was also sick of thinking they were right and that he was a breath away from a meltdown. He needed to get away for his own sanity.

"I'm going to miss you." Lukas finally picked up the envelope and tapped it on the desk.

"I'm going to miss you, too."

Lukas grunted. "Try and sound sincere. Leave a forwarding address."

JT forced out a smile. "I don't want you to tell anyone where I'm going."

"Even Mitch?"

"*Especially* Mitch." The last thing JT needed was Mitch storming back into his life. "Oh, and one more thing."

Lukas scowled at JT across his desk. "Yes?"

"My name's not JT anymore. It's Jacob Tyler. JT died when Riley stuck a knife into my sister's gut.".

be the one to talk first. He always did the talking for the team.

Jake scowled at him, noting the flecks of silver in his jet-black hair that hadn't been there before, and the deeper lines around his midnight-blue eyes. At thirty-four, he was two years older than Jake and the extra maturity suited him. Jake did his best to ignore the effect the rumbling voice had on his senses, and the way he itched to run his fingers through the closely-cropped hair. He knew that hair, the contradiction of soft strands and sharp prickles from the sheared ends. "Why are you here, Mitch? The agreement was I got left alone."

"Riley escaped this morning."

For a brief second Jake closed his eyes, wishing Mitch hadn't said those words. But the second he'd spotted his old team Jake knew why they were in his bar. Lukas wouldn't have betrayed his location for any other reason, especially not to Mitch. He opened his eyes and nodded at the man who'd just turned his life upside down again. "Thanks for telling me. You can go now."

"No can do, JT. We're here to protect you." One of the other men spoke for the first time. "It's good to see you again, bud. Nice place you've got here."

Jake gritted his teeth and tried to smile at the man with the shaved head and scruff of dark-blond beard. "Thanks. It's good to see you, too, Si," he lied, "but I don't need you here. I don't need your protection."

"If he finds you, you're dead." Mitch's voice was so cold Jake would have shivered if he'd been remotely intimidated.

"The cops can deal with Riley, and if you stay away from me he's got no reason to find me. I'm out of this life now."

"You can't be that naïve?" Mitch snapped.

They glared at each other, neither giving way. Jake met Mitch's dark blue depths and tension crackled in the air—as it always had between the two of them. Previous encounters like this had led to X-rated endings.

Si coughed and got to his feet. "Guys, let's get a drink and leave these two to talk. Seriously, dude," he said, nudging Jake as he passed him. "You've got antelope heads on the walls?" He didn't wait for an answer.

If Jake had been watching he'd have laughed at the speed at which Si and the others left the table. But he wasn't. As he opened his mouth to speak, his phone rang.

"It's Lukas." Mitch leaned back against the scuffed leather seat. He seemed content to wait.

Jake pressed his lips together and dug out his phone. "How the hell did you get this number?" he snapped into the speaker.

"JT." Lukas sounded wary—and so he fucking well should—Jake was going to take a long time to forgive him for breaking his confidence.

"He's dead," Jake snapped.

"And yet here you are." The wariness was gone and replaced with outright exasperation. That Jake was familiar with.

"I'm. Jacob. Tyler. JT. Is. Dead. And how the hell did you get this number?" Jake enunciated each word with a snap.

Lukas huffed in his ear. "Don't be a fucking ass, JT, Jacob—whatever. The team is going to take you into protective custody until he's caught."

Jake barked out an incredulous laugh at Lukas' expectation that he would snap to attention. No fucking way. He'd left those days long behind him. "You've got to be fucking kidding me?"

"I wish I was," Lukas said. "Riley escaped three days ago and he's on his way."

"You don't know that."

"They found the address of the bar on a scrap of paper

under his mattress in his cell. We don't know how he found out, but he's coming for you."

"That still doesn't mean—" Jake stopped as Mitch plucked the phone out of his hand. "Gimme my phone back."

"We're here now. He'll be fine," Mitch rumbled to Lukas. "We're gonna lockdown the bar." Jake attempted to grab the phone but Mitch did a two-step out of his reach. "Yeah, he's pissed, but he'll get over it."

"No, I fucking won't," Jake growled. "No one is locking down my bar. You can walk out of here right now."

Mitch glared down at him. Down. Christ, as angry as Jake was, he'd never forgotten how Mitch seemed to surround him, and how much he'd liked it. Howie, Jake's co-owner of the bar was huge, much bigger than Jake and even Mitch, but he didn't have the presence Mitch had. Mitch walked into a room and everything stopped; especially Jake's heart.

"No." Mitch stepped into Jake's personal space.

Jake told his heart and dick to back the fuck off and scowled up at him. He wasn't going to be intimidated by his ex-lover. "I don't want you here."

"You seem to think you have a choice," Mitch snapped. "You don't. Lukas sent us here to protect you and that's what we're gonna do."

"Mitch, I'm in a bar on the edge of a small town in Wyoming surrounded by vets and ex-cops. Even if he finds me, they'll have my back."

Mitch didn't look impressed. "You don't know that."

"Yeah, he does," Carl said. "Jake takes care of us and we look after him and Howie." There was a rumble of agreement around the bar. "I don't know who you are, mister, but Jake don't want you here, so I suggest you leave before we throw you out."

Jake groaned inwardly as conversation in the bar died. Si,

Del and Ruiz looked over, ready for action at a word from Mitch. Jake saw the tension as Carl and his friends got to their feet. He had to head this off before it went south.

"Everyone just relax. I used to work with Mitch and the boys way back." He looked around, making sure to lock eyes with Carl and those liable to kick off first.

"Did you go AWOL, Jake? Are they here to take you back?"

Jake rolled his eyes as Doug, the bar's clown, spoke up. "No, Doug. I didn't go AWOL."

"Didn't you?" Mitch muttered under his breath.

Jake shot him a hard look before he repeated, "We're all fine, boys." It took a second but when Carl sat down, the others followed him and conversation started again, if a little tentatively. Jake expelled a deep breath. "Follow me into the back. We need to talk in private." He turned on his heel, not waiting to see if Mitch followed him. Howie shot them both a worried look as Jake led Mitch around the end of the long, dark mahogany bar. He smiled reassuringly at his partner. "Call me if there's any trouble," Jake said, with a nod to Si, Del and Ruiz.

"As if we would," Si protested.

Jake and Mitch snorted at the same time and, for a moment they shared a grin, remembering previous occasions when Si had denied he had anything to do with fights that had mysteriously broken out when he was around.

The smile swiftly slid off Jake's face and he carried on toward the small room he used as an office. It was barely bigger than a closet but he spent little time in there.

Jake ushered Mitch in and shut the door. As he turned to face him, only lightning reflexes stopped him getting more than a graze on the jaw as Mitch punched him. "What the fuck?" He stumbled back against the desk, the edge catching him painfully against his lower thighs.

"Are you okay?" Howie yelled.

"Fine! It's okay!" Jake shouted to stop anyone running in. "What the hell did you do that for?" he spat, rubbing his jaw.

"You deserve that," Mitch snarled. "And more for what you put me through. You walked out and left me without a word. Not one fucking word! Do you know what I went through? Did you even fucking care?"

Jake bit back the angry words brewing on his lips. He did deserve it. He'd been so lost in his own rage and grief after Sharon's murder that he'd walked away from everything after his meeting with Lukas. He never even went to the home he and Mitch shared to collect his belongings. "I'm sorry."

"You're... sorry?" Mitch stared at him, his expression furious. "You're sorry? Is that it? Is that all you've got to say for yourself?"

Jake sighed and perched on his desk. His jaw stung like a bitch but he wasn't going to give Mitch the satisfaction of rubbing it again. "Is there anything I can say that'll make you feel better?"

"You could at least fucking try."

"Keep your voice down or we'll have the whole fucking bar in here. You think you and the team are hard bastards? You haven't met Carl." The retired Marine was a pussycat compared to these men but Mitch didn't need to know that. Jake searched in his top drawer for Tylenol. He could feel the beginnings of a headache behind his eyes. Mitch grunted but at least he shut up. "How did Riley escape?" Jake asked.

"The ambulance he was in crashed. The guards were knocked out."

Jake grimaced at the taste as he swallowed the pills dry. "Why was he in an ambulance?"

"Stomach pains," Mitch said. "The medics diagnosed suspected appendicitis."

"Was the ambulance hijacked deliberately?" Riley was a resourceful operative and Jake wouldn't put it past him to organize his escape.

Mitch shook his head. "From what we can tell it was a genuine accident. A Chevy burst a tire and skidded out of control into the ambulance's path. They couldn't avoid it. The EMTs are in the hospital and the Chevy driver died at the scene. The guards have cuts and bruises and one has a fractured arm. No sign of Riley."

"Have ERs and clinics been notified?"

"Yeah. So far no one with his description has come in for stomach pains or injuries. One thing you ought to know though."

"Yeah?"

"He was the one who called 911."

Jake laughed although there was no humor in it. "Typical Riley."

Mitch hummed. "Not like it's the first time he's stopped to help someone out."

Riley had always been the one to triage a member of team in the field, or insist they carried a three-hundred-pound man in cardiac arrest to the nearest hospital, despite the fact they'd miss their evac by helping him, and that the dude had been shooting at them five minutes before. Riley's priorities were always skewed.

Jake shook his head. He didn't want to think about Riley like that. He'd murdered his sister. That's all he needed to remember. His beautiful, precious baby sister. "Even if he does come here I can take care of myself," he said.

Mitch huffed impatiently, a sure sign he was still angry. "We're not having this argument again, are we? Lukas told the unit to protect you and that's what we're doing."

"Why you? Why this unit?" Jake's voice was barely above a whisper.

"Because he thinks you're still one of us." Mitch shrugged. "And so do they." He made a stabbing gesture with his finger toward the door.

"And you?"

"You stopped being one of us the second you walked away," Mitch said, the sneer still plastered to his face, but the hurt in his eyes told a different tale. You walked away from me.

At least Jake knew where he stood now. Mitch didn't want anything to do with him. Jake bit back the disappointment in his gut as he stood. It was for the best. He was the one who'd left. "Let's get one thing straight. I'm not running away. You want to catch the fucker? You do it here."

"But—"

"He's not driving me out of my home."

Mitch shook his head. "You're not safe here. If we take you to a safe house until we catch him.... JT, be reasonable."

Jake got into Mitch's space, relishing the anger and uncertainty he saw on his face. Oh yeah, he'd missed this; missed the sparks between them that had flown every day as they lived, loved, worked and fucked together. "I am staying here. End of. And it's Jake."

His expression dark and stormy, Mitch stared down at him, so close his muscled chest brushed Jake's. Jake watched the tic jump under Mitch's left eye, a sure sign he was angry. "You know the risks. Why are you being so damn stupid?"

"He stole everything from me," Jake said. "He's not having my bar, too."

The tic jumped uncontrollably for a few seconds. "He didn't steal me... us. You were the one who threw that away."

Jake couldn't deny the truth in Mitch's heated words. He took a step back only to be halted by the edge of his desk. Crossing his arms in defiance he said firmly, "I'm staying here. Like it, or fuck off."

Mitch threw his hands up in despair. "Fine. But you do as I say. Riley's a dangerous bastard and he was trained by the best."

"I trained him," Jake snapped.

"Exactly."

The unexpected compliment did strange things to Jake's heart but he refused to back down. He glared at Mitch. "Keep your boys out of my way and we'll be fine."

"They were your boys once," Mitch pointed out.

That stung but Jake snapped back. "That was in another lifetime. Now I've got my bar with Howie."

The tic danced a fandango. "He's your partner/lover... what?"

"None of your business." Jake was perversely pleased to see the muscles in Mitch's jaw tighten.

"I need to know if Howie's gonna be a problem," Mitch said.

"Why should he be?" Jake asked. "Riley's after me, not him."

"What if Riley decides to attack someone who's important to you?"

"You think he would do that?" Jake had never considered that possibility, although up to thirty minutes ago, he'd never considered the possibility of Riley escaping jail or being in the same room as Mitch again.

Mitch sighed and scrubbed a hand through his hair. "Who knows what the fuck he's going to do? We need to consider all options."

"If he's going for people I care about, he's just as likely to attack you." Mitch blinked, his long dark lashes sweeping over his eyes and, too late, Jake realized what he'd said. "Cared about, that's what I meant."

Mitch raised an eyebrow. "Sure about that?"

Jake had no fucking idea what he was sure about, except getting the hell out of his office before he made a total ass of himself. He flung open the door, gritting his teeth as he heard the soft snicker from behind him.

CHAPTER 2

The bar was quiet—too quiet. It was never this quiet, even at the start of the day when his regulars stumbled in for a breakfast of hash browns and bacon. There was always someone yelling and cussing, but now conversations continued in slow hushed voices and no one looked Jake in the eye. He stalked over to the bar where Howie was polishing the mirrored wall. It had already been cleaned that morning so Howie had obviously been looking for something to do. Jake fixed Howie's reflection with a glare. "What happened?"

Howie turned; his mouth pressed together so tightly there was a thin white line around his mouth. "Nothing."

"Where are they?" Jake demanded. Si, Del and Ruiz were nowhere to be seen. Nor was Carl.

"I don't know." Howie refused to meet Jake's gaze.

"You're a shit poker player," Jake growled. "Where are they?"

"Out back with Carl, Doug and the boys."

"Oh fuck, are you insane? Si and the team will kill them." Jake rushed out the back door of the bar and stopped dead. "What the hell is going on here?"

Seated at the old wooden table, Si and Carl looked up, intense expressions on their faces.

"Shop talk," Si said, indicating the M4 assault rifle between them.

Jake stabbed a finger toward the M4. "Don't you dare use

that in my bar!"

"Where's the rest of the team?" Mitch asked. He'd come up behind Jake without him noticing.

"Doug's showing them the access points to the bar," Si said. "He's infantry. Carl's a Marine."

Jake's hackles rose at Mitch's derisive grunt and he spun on his heel to stare at him. "I told you I didn't need you here."

Si glanced between them. "Are you two gonna get over this pissing contest or do I have to get Lukas down here?" His tone indicated he was a heartbeat away from calling the section leader if Jake and Mitch didn't sort out their shit.

Jake ground his teeth together in frustration. "There's nothing to get over. I don't need you." Carl coughed, and Jake looked at him in surprise. "What?"

"If Riley's as good as everyone says he is, you shouldn't be so hasty to dismiss your friends, Jake."

Jake stared at him. "They ain't my friends." Then he caught the wounded look on Si's face. He didn't dare turn around to see Mitch's expression.

Carl scowled at him. "They've come three thousand miles to protect your ungrateful ass. You think these men aren't your friends? They're family, boy, and you'd better step up and accept their help, because next time you might find yourself in trouble and on your own." He got to his feet and held out his hand to Si. "Good to talk to you, Si. You're always welcome for the pot roast." He disappeared back inside, leaving Jake with the two people he'd just insulted.

Mitch shoved Jake toward the table. "Sit the fuck down, JT—Jake—and we'll talk."

Jake opened his mouth to argue and then shut it again. He huffed and sat next to Si, not wanting to be close to Mitch, then realized he'd have to look Mitch in the face.

Del and Ruiz returned and sat down next to Mitch. Jake

studied them; noting lines that hadn't been there when he'd left, gray streaking their hair. They studied him just as intently, a wary look in their eyes. When the silence stretched on Jake thought he ought to say something.

"What now?"

"You gonna co-operate?" Mitch growled.

Jake knuckled his eyes. "Do I gotta choice?"

Si shook his head. "No."

"Okay, then I'll co-operate, but I'm staying here." Jake wasn't being shoved out of his home.

Mitch fixed him with his deep blue gaze. "We'll protect you."

Jake didn't want protecting but he knew he didn't have a choice. "What are your orders regarding Riley?"

"To take him back," Mitch said.

"Dead or alive?" Jake asked. He saw a muscle twitch in Del's jaw.

"Alive unless he makes it impossible." Si answered for the team.

Jake had expected as much. He got to his feet, brushing off his ass. "I need to get back to work."

"You won't even know we're here," Si said cheerfully.

Jake snorted at Si's blatant horse-pucky. "You'll want feeding I assume?" He rolled his eyes at the nods from everyone except Mitch. "The first one's on the house. After that you pay. I know how much you eat."

"Send the check to Lukas," Ruiz said.

Si and Del burst out laughing, and even Mitch smiled. Jake knew why. He had more chance of getting expenses out of the Pope.

"I'll give you a hand." Del stood and dusted his ass.

Jake didn't object. Del and he had produced the team's meals many times. "I suppose one of you is gonna be up my ass at all times?"

Del grunted in assent. "Lukas' orders. He's livid about Riley's escape. You should've heard him when he got the news. I thought he was going to have an aneurysm."

"He hasn't changed." Jake chuckled but that died when Del caught his arm and they stopped just shy of the bar.

"You're wrong," Del said.

"About what?"

"About not changing." His dark gaze held Jake's. "We all have since Sharon's death, especially Lukas and Mitch. Losing you and Riley ripped the heart out of the team."

He didn't sound accusing and Jake didn't bristle—much. Walking away from his lover, his family—because his team were as much family as blood—had been the hardest thing he'd ever done.

"I had to go."

Del slid his hand up and squeezed Jake's shoulder. "I know you did. Probably better than any of them out there. I left the Marines, remember?" Del had been a late addition to the team, a new recruit after Del's unit had come under attack in Afghanistan. He'd arrived a year before Sharon died. "We don't blame you for leaving, JT... Jake, but leaving without a word? I thought Mitch was gonna have a breakdown. Me and the boys watched him 24/7 for weeks in case he decided to eat his weapon."

Jake flinched, guilt eating him up. He hadn't been thinking about Mitch. All he'd been thinking about was his best friend standing over his sister with the bloody knife in his hand. It had haunted him day and— "You knew about us?"

Del rolled his eyes. "We all knew, dipshit. We had a pool running on when you were gonna shove Mitch out of the closet."

"I really thought we'd managed to keep it quiet."

"You're an idiot, Jake Tyler. Like I said, Mitch was on the edge for a long time. Don't think this is easy for him because it isn't. Lukas debated sending another team and not telling Mitch, but he knew if it got back to him, Mitch would gut him."

"I'm sorry." The threat of tears prickled behind Jake's eyes and throat. *Christ, I have to get a grip.* There was nothing he could do about the past.

Del's expression was kind but somber. "It's not me you need to apologize to, Jake."

"Yes, I do. I walked out on all of you, not just Mitch."

"You were hurting." Del said. "Sharon's death ripped the guts from all of us."

Jake sighed. He'd left his family while they were fractured and no amount of reassurances from Del could change that. "Why didn't you get replacements for the team?" he asked.

Del shrugged. "We tried but no one fit, you know? Everyone that Lukas forced on us wasn't you... or Riley. In the end Lukas gave up, but the team still isn't right. We're missing you."

Howie suddenly appeared, his brows knit together, his gaze fixed on Jake. "You okay?"

Okay was a stretch but Howie looked as if he needed reassurance. "I guess," Jake replied. "The boys are gonna be here a while."

Howie nodded, not looking surprised. "They need feeding?"

"I'll do it," Jake said. "We're gonna need to go to the store tomorrow though. They eat a lot."

"One of us will go with you," Del said. "But not Ruiz. He'll eat the chow before you get back here."

He smirked at Jake who returned the gesture, then Jake

caught Howie's crushed expression. Howie was a gentle soul, who only wanted everyone to be happy. When they'd first met in a bar not far from J.T's, Jake had been knotted up inside, angry at everyone and most folk had steered clear of him after their first encounter. Howie hadn't been put off by Jake's angry snarls. If anything, his gentle demeanor had gone a long way to soothing Jake's tortured soul and, when J.T's went up for sale, they both wanted to work together. The only thing Jake couldn't do was return Howie's feelings for him. As much as he liked his partner, Howie wasn't his type. His type was sitting outside with a sullen attitude and a hurt that Jake had put there.

Jake patted Howie's giant bicep then squeezed by to take Del into the kitchen. They spent the next fifteen minutes carving thick slices of bread and filling them with cheese, ham, and turkey, plus salad, pickles and chips.

Jake looked up as Del chuckled. "What's so funny?"

"You still remember the order."

"Too many years of pickles and no pickles to forget," Jake said, slapping the top slice of bread on each one and skewering them with a JT's sandwich pick.

Del shook his head. "You were the only one who got it right."

"That's 'cause the others never bothered to listen." Jake hefted the tray of sandwiches. "Grab the chips."

Del did as he said and followed Jake out to the bar. Mitch and Ruiz had found a corner table and were looking over maps. Si was nowhere to be seen. Come to that, neither was Carl. Jake frowned, wondering what was going on between them. Someone had stuck a cheesy eighties ballad on the jukebox.

Ruiz pushed the maps aside as Jake approached, ignoring Mitch's annoyed growl. "'Bout time, man."

"You shoulda come and helped," Del snapped as he handed Mitch a plate.

"You're better in the kitchen than I am." Ruiz virtually snatched his plate out of Jake's hands. "*Madre de dios*, this is manna from heaven."

"It's a turkey sandwich, dude." Jake chuckled as Ruiz drooled over the food.

"Yeah, but *you* made it." Anything else Ruiz was going to say was lost as he stuffed half the sandwich in his mouth.

Del made a disgusted noise. "Jesus, you're a pig." He growled as Ruiz flipped him off and carried on chewing noisily.

Jake shook his head. "Nothing's changed. You're still assholes."

"Did you expect anything different?" Mitch leaned back in his chair and raised a challenging eyebrow at Jake.

"You coulda taught them manners."

Si grunted. "You gotta have fucking manners first. We follow our leader."

Mitch flipped him off and Ruiz started to laugh, but he choked on a mouthful of sandwich.

Jake left the others to deal with Ruiz choking and spluttering. Howie waved a hand at him as he returned to the bar. Jake smiled at him, then caught sight of the tightness around Howie's eyes and mouth and the smile slid off his face. He leaned over the bar. "Wanna talk about it?"

Howie refused to look him in the eye and just wiped the same small circle of the polished bar over and over. "What's there to talk about?"

Fuck, it had turned into a craptastic day and now he was going to have to have the conversation he'd been avoiding for months. Jake held back a sigh and rubbed his temples as he looked around the room. "Moose, mind the bar for a while."

“Sure thing, Jake.” Moose, one of the regulars, ambled over and took Howie’s place behind the bar. He was large and rangy, hence his nickname, and he’d been a state trooper until a routine stop had ended with Moose in intensive care for a month after he’d been viciously attacked.

Jake hustled Howie out the back, grabbing their jackets on the way and pointed to the seat. Howie sat down reluctantly, like Jake was forcing him to walk on hot coals. Jake parked himself opposite and studied his partner, noting the sadness in his eyes. Jake didn’t know what to say, how to restore the balance between them. “Talk to me, Howie.”

Howie looked like he was chewing on glass. “So these are the guys you used to work with?”

“Now you’ve met them.”

“You didn’t tell me about Mitch.” Howie looked up and his hurt was there for Jake to see.

Jake had given Howie a redacted version of his past but he’d never been able to talk about the man who still had his heart.

“What’s to tell? It was over a long time ago.” Jake tried to brazen it out but Howie just shook his head.

“Have you told *him* that? Have you told yourself?” Howie said. He looked away from Jake. “I don’t have a chance, do I?”

What the hell was he supposed to say to that? Jake bit his lip. “I’m sorry, Howie.”

“Nothing to be sorry about.” Howie pushed his hair back again and got to his feet. “You never promised anything. It was me. I was stupid enough to.... I’m gonna go back inside. You know what Moose is like when anyone gives him money.”

Howie left without another word and Jake thunked his head on the rough wooden table. He’d probably have a forehead full of splinters but at this point he didn't care. Then the bench and table wobbled and Jake cursed under his breath. Hell, he couldn't even have a meltdown in peace.

"Rough day?"

Jake didn't raise his head at the rumbling question. He didn't want to look into Mitch's eyes and drown in their dark depths. "What do you think?"

"Want to talk about it?"

That was the last thing Jake wanted to do. He managed to spit out a, "Go 'way."

"Can't do that. You need an escort, remember?"

Jake did look up at that point. "Where were you just now? Did you hear all that?"

Mitch had the grace to look apologetic. "I did. I made sure Howie didn't see me when he went inside."

Jake knocked the table again with his forehead. He'd be more than happy to stay in this position for the rest of the day.

"You never told him about me." Mitch didn't sound angry although there was an edge of something—maybe curiosity.

"No. I couldn't share.... I just couldn't," Jake mumbled.

Mitch nodded. "Did you know about his feelings for you?"

"Howie's a great guy."

"That's not what I asked."

"I knew," Jake admitted. "I kinda ignored it, because...."

"He's not your type but you didn't want to hurt him."

Jake bristled at the smug satisfaction in Mitch's voice. "You don't know that."

"Yeah, I do," Mitch said.

Jake didn't bother to deny it because of course Mitch knew Jake's type. From the first moment they'd laid eyes on each other, it had been obvious they pushed each other everywhere it counted. He sat up and looked into Mitch's eyes. "Don't hurt him."

"I'm not that guy."

Jake caught the hurt in Mitch's voice but he wasn't going to apologize. Howie deserved better than that. "I know you're not, but Howie isn't like us. He's gentle and vulnerable."

"You like him," Mitch said quietly.

It wasn't a question. "Just not in the way he wants."

Mitch nodded but the smugness had gone to be replaced by something gentler. He'd always had the ability to empathize with people. He wasn't the hard-ass most people thought he was. Jake corrected himself. Mitch was a hard-ass, when it counted. That's what made him a good leader. He tempered the rough edges of the rest of the team. Jake tried not to think about the fact that he included himself as a member of the team. "I'll tell the others to mind their manners around him."

"Thanks." Jake furrowed his brow. "Do you really think Riley's coming here?"

"I'm sure of it. He's never stopped protesting his innocence."

"So why come to me?" Riley must know what Jake would do if he ever saw him again. Jake had yelled at the judge in open court that he'd kill Riley if he ever went free. The judge had nearly jailed Jake for the outburst.

"Because you're the one person he needs to convince. If you believe he didn't kill Sharon, then everyone else will."

"But I caught him with the knife. I know he did it."

Mitch shrugged. "I didn't say it was logical, JT, Jake." He quickly corrected himself and then frowned as if it annoyed him.

Jake sighed as he sat back. "I need to get back inside. I've got the accounts to do. I hate paperwork."

"You should get Ruiz to do them," Mitch said. "You know

how good he is with figures."

"He'd kill me." Jake grinned at Mitch who blinked, as if startled by his amusement.

"Even more reason to get him to do something useful."

"You guys catch my psychotic ex-brother-in-law then Ruiz can do my accounts."

"You're on."

Mitch grinned back at him then his grin faded to become something deeper, more intense. Jake felt like one word, one twitch and they would both go up in flames. Fuck, he didn't need this now. He'd left that part of his life behind.

Footsteps broke the spell between them.

"You forgot your chow, Mitch." Del broke the spell as he held out a plate to Mitch. Jake drew in a shaky breath and Del looked between them. "Have I interrupted something?"

"No." Jake bolted inside like the hounds of hell were nipping at his heels. The last thing he needed was complications. Especially not in the form of the only man who haunted his dreams.

Howie avoided Jake's gaze as he re-entered the bar. Jake knew he was going to have to put out some serious fires when this horse-shit was over. The team would leave and Jake would be left to pick up the pieces of his life again.

Jake cursed Riley's name long and hard. Once more the man he'd called best friend, team mate and brother-in-law had carved chaos into his life. "I'm gonna kill you, Riley Ward. And this time they can't stop me."

CHAPTER 3

The bar was empty aside from Mitch and Jake. He'd almost manhandled Carl and Doug out the door, with the understanding they would be back first thing in the morning. He half-expected to see them, shotguns at the ready, outside the main door as the sun rose. Howie was in the kitchen washing the glasses and clearing up. Despite Jake urging him to leave, Howie had refused to go home to his small one-story about half a mile from the bar. Jake was the only one who lived in a couple of rooms at the back of the bar. He couldn't afford his own place, but he'd never needed much beyond a place to lay his head and take a shower. All his waking moments were spent in the bar so he didn't need a place to relax.

Si, Del and Ruiz were guarding the access points to the building, which left Mitch and Jake staring awkwardly at each other across one of the battered wooden tables. Si had told them to "Fucking sort it!" before the evening was over. Mitch had snarled at him but Si just flipped him off and walked out, leaving them to it.

Jake stared at the coffee mug in front of him, filled with a steaming dark brew. Where did he start?

"Have there been any sightings of Riley?"

Mitch shook his head. "I called Lukas fifteen minutes ago. There's been nothing since Riley escaped from the ambulance. We've got no clue where he is, or how he's traveling. He's been in Central Prison in Raleigh, North

Carolina for the past six months and he has to get to Wyoming."

Jake frowned. "North Carolina? I thought he was in Texas. Why did he move?" *Lukas should have told me, dammit!*

"There was some trouble. One of the inmates tried to shank him. Riley took exception to that and nearly killed the guy."

"Pity he didn't succeed," Jake muttered.

Mitch looked confused. "Which one?"

"Either. Both. So why did they move him?"

"I don't know. I can find out."

It was Jake's turn to shake his head. "It doesn't matter."

"I'm surprised Riley was involved in any trouble, although he was always a ruthless bastard," Mitch mused.

"Maybe he didn't have a choice." Riley had been ruthless only when necessary. At the end of the day he'd been content to go home to his wife. He'd had no friends beyond the team and their partners.

"Who knows what prison does to a man?" Mitch said. "If he's in North Carolina he's got—what—two thousand miles to get here? If this *was* an accident he won't have fake ID. He can't fly, so his only option is hitch-hiking. If he's wearing his prison gear he won't get far."

Jake looked skeptical. "Riley's resourceful. Are you telling me he didn't swap clothes with one of the guards?"

"If he didn't, he'll find clothes another way," Mitch agreed.

"He's not going to stick to the main highways. Is he going to hitch-hike or steal a vehicle?"

It was like old times with the two of them sitting over coffee, discussing details of the operation and planning their next move. Jake grabbed his coffee mug, taking a long chug to stop himself from blurting out something stupid. The last thing he needed was to give away how much he liked being with Mitch again.

"How many clinics and hospitals are there from here to North Carolina?" Mitch didn't seem to notice Jake's inward freak-out. "If he's in pain he's gonna struggle to get here."

"Which makes me wonder if that whole accident was a set-up."

Mitch nodded. "As you said, Riley's resourceful. If he got a message to people he *could* organize it."

Deep in thought, Jake got up to fetch the coffee pot. Once he'd topped off their mugs and returned to his seat, he said, "We should make a few calls. Perhaps someone's heard something."

"I'll get Lukas on it."

Jake waited while Mitch sent a text, presumably to their section leader. His *former* section leader he amended silently. He drank his coffee and waited for Mitch to focus his attention on their conversation again. When Mitch looked up, Jake said, "If Riley's got a fake ID he could fly here."

"In which case he could be here now."

"He could. Fuck." Jake's stomach churned at the thought. He wasn't ready to face his sister's murderer yet. Or ever. The only time Jake had sworn to face his ex-brother-in-law was when they stuck the needle in his arm, but the bastard District Attorney had taken the death penalty off the table.

"We'll be prepared," Mitch assured him. "He won't get near you." He reached over and placed his large hand over Jake's, warm and comforting, his olive skin a sharp contrast to Jake's. His coloring was much paler, a sign of the Irish heritage somewhere way back in his ancestry.

Jake looked at their two hands and Mitch's larger, blunt fingers. He remembered the first day Mitch had touched him with more than an impersonal interest; the feel of Mitch's hand on his cheek, trailing his jawline and whispering down his spine. Jake had learned to crave that touch. He would wake up seeking it and not be able to sleep without it. In the first alcohol-fueled months after he abandoned his life, it was the touch of Mitch's hands that Jake missed the most.

He extracted his hand from under Mitch's. He couldn't afford to indulge that weakness again. Jake looked at Mitch and, sure enough, the tic under Mitch's left eye twitched, but he didn't say anything.

The tension between them crackled, only to be broken as the outside door banged open and Si strolled in, blowing on his hands, followed by Howie from the kitchen not more than two seconds later.

Jake welcomed the interruption. He couldn't afford to let his heart distract him. This was an operation, not a second chance and he and Mitch both needed to remember that.

"It's colder than a witch's tit out there," Si said, rubbing his hands together.

"Bring the boys back in," Mitch ordered. "You can't see dick out there anyway. We'll all sleep in the bar tonight. Howie, you should go home."

Howie shook his head. The stubborn set to his jaw something that Jake was only too familiar with. "I'm not leaving Jake."

"I'll be fine, Howie. I've got the best to protect me," Jake assured him, and noticed Si preen and Mitch's slight smile.

"I don't care. I'm staying."

Jake opened his mouth to argue with his partner but to his surprise Si intervened. "It's okay, Jake. I'll look after Howie."

Si focused his attention on Howie. "Anything happens, and I mean *anything*, you go down to the basement and you don't come up until I tell you it's safe to. Do you understand?"

Howie blinked at the order then he nodded once, and again. "I understand."

Jake stared, his mouth open. Out of the corner of his eye he caught a similarly shocked expression on Mitch's face. This was a new side to his teammate that neither of them had seen before.

Si seemed oblivious to the shock on their faces as he said, "I'll get Del and Ruiz. All our gear is in the SUV. We'll bring that in, too." He left, breaking the spell.

Jake glanced at Mitch. "I guess you're gonna want me and Howie sleeping in here too?"

"We'll all take turns to take watch. No point wearing ourselves out tonight. If Riley's on his way, my gut tells me he won't be here before tomorrow." Mitch looked at Howie. "I don't want you here. You're untrained and a liability—"

"I can help," Howie burst out, but he went silent when Jake got to his feet. "Jake, tell him—"

Jake held his hand up to forestall the angry words obviously gathering on Howie's lips. "Howie, buddy, do what Si says. Any issues go down into the basement. You'll be safest there."

"But—" Howie tried once more but Jake interrupted him.

"I told you. I've got the best here."

Mitch glared at Jake. "You were the best."

"Let's hope that still holds true," he managed.

"It'd better," Mitch growled and Jake shivered under his heated gaze, suppressing the urge to jump to attention and salute. Mitch had always had that effect on him.

Jake focused his attention on Howie, knowing his partner was a hair's breadth from a meltdown. "You just listen to Si and Mitch, okay? You'll be fine." He squeezed Howie's forearm. "Let's get bedding down for you and me. I assume you're not letting me sleep in my bedroom?" The last was aimed at Mitch, who stared at Howie with a faintly hostile expression on his face.

"You assume right. We're all sleeping in the bar, with a watch all night."

"I'll get sleeping bags and pillows. Howie, you clear a space for us in here."

Howie nodded without speaking and began to push chairs and tables to the sides.

By the time Jake had returned, the bar was clear and the team's mats and sleeping bags were laid out. Jake handed Howie a sleeping bag, pillow and a mat, and Si waved him over to a space near him. Howie looked bemused by the interest the big guy was showing in him, but Jake knew Howie was in safe hands. Si took his responsibilities seriously.

There was one space left for Jake and he didn't need to be a genius to know it would be beside Mitch. That's the way they had always paired off: him and Mitch, Si and Riley, and Del and Ruiz.

"You and I'll take first watch," Mitch said.

Jake nodded. That was usual, too. They waited for the other men to settle down and took their places; Mitch by the window of the main door to the bar, Jake by the window at the back of the bar. Jake switched off the lights when Mitch gave the signal and he settled in for a long, boring, three-hour shift.

As he'd expected nothing disturbed them and Mitch quietly shook Del and Ruiz awake at 2 a.m. Jake was glad to snuggle into his sleeping bag and closed his eyes. It was only moments later when Mitch settled down beside him for the first time in too long. It was strange to have him there; so close yet so far. Jake only needed to roll over and he would be able to kiss him. He didn't, but the knowledge that he could was somehow comforting and he fell asleep to the sound of rumbling snores, and Mitch's steady breathing.

A low buzz of conversation disturbed Jake's slumber and he raised his head, blinking to try and focus in the dark, but it was only Del and Ruiz swapping with Si and Howie. *Howie?* Jake sat up fully but Mitch dragged him down against him.

"I agreed to this last night. Howie insisted on doing something," Mitch hissed in his ear.

"But—"

"Just tonight. 'Kay?"

It wasn't okay. It was far from okay. Howie wasn't trained. He could get them all killed if he missed something.

"Moose is watching the back from his truck," Mitch whispered, his hot breath tickling the sensitive skin behind Jake's ear. "Carl and Doug took the earlier shifts. They were gonna do it anyway."

Jake relaxed against Mitch. "You could've told me."

"Sorry."

Mitch didn't sound apologetic, but it was the middle of the night and Jake was too tired to argue. He would pick it up again in the morning. Mitch didn't move away and Jake fell asleep with Mitch spooning him, the most relaxed he'd been in years.

Jake had forgotten the deliveries due at 7 a.m and Howie shook him awake, signing to him about the delivery of beer waiting outside. He tried to slide free of the sleeping bag without disturbing Mitch, but he wasn't surprised when Mitch's eyes blinked open.

"Is he here?" Mitch's voice was gruff with sleep, but he sat up, unzipping his sleeping bag.

"No, just the beer delivery. Go back to sleep." Jake stood up, unsurprised when Mitch followed him.

Mitch frowned as he peered out of the back window at the two men waiting beside the delivery truck. "Do you recognize them?"

Jake looked over his shoulder. "Yeah, they're both regulars."

"Si and Del, check the truck. Try not to upset them. Jake and Howie, you stay here until Si gives the all clear."

The two operatives nodded, easing out of the front door to walk around the side of the building, checking for any surprises before they engaged the delivery guys in conversation. The men looked surprised and a little suspicious at Si's request to check the truck, but whatever he said must have worked because they stood back to allow him and Del to check the vehicle. A few minutes later, Si gave a thumbs-up to the back window.

Mitch nodded to Jake and Howie. "Okay."

Jake joined Si, Del and the two delivery men. The older man, a black guy who always reminded Jake of Morgan Freeman, looked quizzically at him.

"Everything okay, Jake?"

Jake did his best to smile. "All good, Lionel. Just had some odd phone calls is all. Can't be too careful, y'know?"

Lionel's gaze flicked to Del and Si then back at Jake. "You always call in the big guns for dumb phone calls?"

"I know the right people," Jake said. "Now they can put their hand to something useful and help me with the delivery."

"I thought we were the big guns," Si protested.

Without saying a word Jake handed him a barrel and Si grumbled, but he followed Howie down the steps into the basement of the bar. Jake grinned at Lionel and took another barrel, handing it to Del.

Lionel stared, obviously uncertain, but after a moment he shrugged. “Delivery will sure go a lot quicker with all this extra help.”

When they’d gone, the four men trooped into the bar. Howie grabbed Jake’s sleeve and held him back a moment. “Jake, I saw something last night.”

Jake frowned at him. “You did? Why didn’t you tell Si?”

“Because I think it was Moose. He lit up a cigarette and I saw his face.” Howie looked at Jake shrewdly. “Was it Moose?”

Jake nodded. “Mitch said Moose was there. I’m gonna ream him out for doing something so stupid.”

“Lighting the cigarette?”

“If you saw him and Riley’s close by, he will have, too.”

Howie nodded, seemingly not upset by Jake’s comment. “Do you want me to start breakfast?”

“Yeah. Hash browns and bacon, and you can use up the last of the eggs. We gotta go to the store today anyway. These guys can eat.” Jake took a mental inventory of the pantry’s contents. “I hope they won’t be here long or we’ll go bankrupt.”

“Should we leave here?”

“*I* shouldn’t, but I think you’re safe. I’ll send Si with you to make sure.”

“He’s scary,” Howie observed.

“Yeah, there’s no denying that. But he’s the best, Howie.” Jake squeezed Howie’s hand where it lay on his sleeve.

Howie nodded and disappeared into the kitchen, leaving Jake to join the others in the bar. Despite the disturbed night, Jake’s nerves buzzed with an excitement he hadn’t felt for years. He thrived on situations like this. It’s why he’d been so good at his job.

"What was all that about?" Mitch asked, nodding in the direction of the kitchen.

"Howie's gonna make us all breakfast. And he saw Moose last night," Jake said.

"Observant of him," Si sounded proud, like he'd had something personal to do with it.

"Moose lit up a smoke in the cab of his truck."

"Stupid idiot." Mitch let out an expletive. "If Howie saw it, Riley sure as hell did."

"I'll talk to Moose, Doug and Carl," Jake said. "If they're going to help we can't have them making such rookie mistakes."

"I'll do it," Mitch said. "They'll probably listen to me. You got any more deliveries today?"

Jake shook his head. "But I've got paperwork to do this morning."

"You go do that." Mitch looked almost relieved to know Jake would be corralled in the tiny office.

"You call me if you hear anything." Jake was reluctant to go, but the accounts had to be done and he knew if he had nothing to do he'd end up in a screaming match with Mitch. Knowing their past had some benefits.

Mitch nodded. "I promise. Now fuck off and let me do my job."

Jake huffed but he vanished into the small office to wrangle the figures into submission.

CHAPTER 4

Instead of concentrating on the accounts, Jake spent most of the morning thinking about another figure he'd like to wrangle. He was sure one of the team guarded the door but he didn't emerge to find out who it was. After two hours of staring blankly at the screen, he could've sworn the damn figures just fucked off and found new columns to rest in. When someone finally knocked at the door, he was almost relieved.

"What do you want?"

There was a momentary hesitation then Si poked his head around the door. "Howie said, as you were doing accounts, you'd need this." He held out a large mug of coffee which Jake virtually leapt across the room to accept. Si's lips twitched. "He also said, if you cussed at me, I should give you a shot of Jack."

"If I cuss at you now do I still get the liquor?" Jake asked hopefully.

Si leaned against the doorframe. "Drink the coffee first."

Jake grumbled but he downed the coffee. It was hot and strong, just as he liked it, and the caffeine burned through his system, waking him up. "Where's my Jack?"

"Mitch says you ain't drinking with a psycho after you."

Jake glared at Si who smirked at him. "Bastard. It's wrong to promise a man and then not deliver."

"You're welcome. You gonna quit hiding in here?"

"I'm not hiding," Jake lied.

Si snorted. "You keep telling yourself that, Skippy."

"I'm *not* hiding. Well, not much. I'm not used to being the target instead of one of the team."

Si pulled up a chair and sat close enough that Jake could smell his spicy cologne. "You're still part of the team."

"But I'm not, am I?" Christ, Jake knew he sounded pathetic.

"We're a team, dumbass." As Jake opened his mouth, Si scowled at him and he closed it again. "Yeah, yeah, I know you fucked off, but you're still part of *my* team. You're more a part of the team than any of those idiots Lukas tried to foist on us."

Jake smirked. "Were they really that bad?"

"You remember Ryan?"

"Eli Ryan?" At Si's nod, Jake started laughing. "How long did he last before Mitch exploded?"

Si grinned at him. "Thirty-five minutes."

Jake laughed harder, imagining Mitch losing it at the poor man. Mitch didn't suffer fools gladly and Ryan might have been a good soldier but he was a lousy operative.

Si chuckled and patted Jake's knee as Jake's laughter subsided. "You know you can talk to me, Jake."

"You turned into Doctor Phil?" Jake looked away, not wanting Si to see how choked up he was.

Si shoved him hard. "You're a real fucker, Jake Tyler."

Jake smirked as he recovered his balance but it didn't last long.

"Is it Howie—or Mitch?" Si asked eventually.

Jake sighed and scrubbed his hand through his hair. "Either. Both. Howie is pissed at me for not telling him about Mitch and for... other things. Mitch is just Mitch. You know what happened there."

"They'll get over it."

Jake blinked at Si's blasé tone. "That's a bit heartless."

Si leaned back in his chair and crossed his ankles. "Mitch still loves you, you stupid fucker. And you love him. Don't try to deny it. You two are hopeless. He spent the whole night watching you in case you vanished from his sight. Bet you didn't know that. Bet you didn't know you reached out for him in your sleep. As for Howie... He's just looking in the wrong direction."

Jake blinked as he processed that information. Mitch had watched over him? *Wait... Wrong direction? What?* His gazed widened as the penny dropped. "You're interested in Howie? You're gay?"

Si shrugged. "I'm bisexual. I like boobs and I like dick. And no, I didn't tell the team for the same reason you and Mitch kept your traps shut. But yeah, I like Howie."

"You've only just met him." Jake frowned. "Howie's not like us, Si. He's gentle. I don't want you playing with his feelings and then fucking off."

"I'm not the one who fucked off," Si pointed out and Jake flinched. "I'm sorry, Jake, but—"

"Yeah, yeah, you're right." Jake waved his hand. "I did, but Howie is my friend. He's a lover, not a fighter."

"Not all of us want fighters," Si said gently. "Some of us just want a warm body and a warm heart to come home to."

Jake studied Si. His friend was a hard-ass. Probably the hardest guy he'd ever met, except for Ruiz, and yet he wanted a gentle giant like Howie? Who knew? "Just be careful. Don't hurt him."

"I can't make any promises but I'll try not to." Si looked uncharacteristically sober and Jake nodded, satisfied for now.

Another knock at the door made them both look up. This time it was Mitch and he didn't look happy.

"Riley's been spotted about five hundred klicks away. He's traveled faster than we'd hoped."

Jake and Si gave each other a resigned look and followed Mitch out of the office. Del and Ruiz, along with Carl, Doug and Moose were gathered around a table.

"You're telling me he was seen and they didn't stop him?" Jake demanded.

"State Troopers saw him at a rest stop but by the time they'd realize it was him he'd taken off in a truck," Del said.

"Stolen?" Jake asked.

"Yeah, the driver left the keys while he went to take a leak."

Ruiz made a derisive snort. "He's evaded road blocks, changed clothes, he's got transport. He's one of us alright. You trained him well, Jake."

Carl cleared his throat. "Are you sure no one's helping him?"

Jake frowned. "Who? Riley's parents are dead and he was an only child."

"Aunts, uncles, cousins? What about a friend? He must have got your address from somewhere." Carl ticked the list off on his fingers.

"The bar's on the internet and *we* were his friends," Jake said as the team shook their heads in unison. They all knew Riley's history. "And he has no family. Riley grew up in foster care. Bounced around from one home to another until he got turned out when he was sixteen. Then he worked and got his GED until he was old enough to join the army."

Carl looked as frustrated as the rest of them. "Maybe it's someone he met in prison."

"I'll get Lukas to check." Mitch fished his cell phone out of his pocket. He walked away, talking rapidly when Lukas answered.

Jake sank down onto the nearest seat, not paying attention to the people talking around them. Why the hell did Riley want to see him? He must know, even if Jake didn't kill him, the team would be waiting for him. Perhaps that's what he wanted—to wipe out his old team in a final act of revenge.

Mitch sat down next to him, his hand sliding down Jake's arm. "How are you doing?"

Jake stared at him helplessly. "Can we have a do-over? When I woke up yesterday life was simple."

"When I woke up yesterday I didn't know where you lived. Today you were next to me when I woke up, where you belong. This isn't Groundhog Day. We don't get do-overs. I don't want to wake up another day without you next to me." Mitch's voice was low and raw with pain, but with an intensity that cut Jake to the quick.

"Mitch—"

He stopped as Mitch slammed his fist on the table. "Don't."

Jake looked up to see everyone staring at them. Mitch growled under his breath and stomped out of the bar. "Sorry," Jake mumbled to the others. He felt so fucking helpless.

"Nothing to be sorry for," Del said. "We've got to close the bar, at least for today. It's not right to put your customers in danger."

"I ain't going anywhere." The set of Carl's jaw was clearly a challenge and Doug nodded his head so vigorously Jake was convinced it was going to topple off his neck.

"Nor me."

"If the bar looks shut it'll alert Riley," Ruiz said. "He's not stupid. He'll know Lukas will have told you."

"I'll get the word out to the regulars." Carl looked at Doug. "We need to make some phone calls."

Jake glanced around at the team. "How did you lot get here?"

Si hefted car keys. "I'll move the SUV. We should have done it last night. If he sees the plates he'll know we're here."

"You can park it in my yard," Howie said.

Jake had been so busy staring at the door Mitch had stormed out of he hadn't noticed Howie had joined them.

Si smiled at Howie. "Is it far?" Howie blinked at the intensity of Si's smile. So did Del and Ruiz, but Si ignored them, focusing on Howie.

"It… it's about half a mile down the road. I'll get the keys."

Howie disappeared into the office, a second before Del turned on Si. "What the fuck, man?"

Si frowned, his light brows knit together over his nose. "You gotta problem with me liking Howie? You want him for yourself?"

"Don't be fucking stupid." Del was the only member of the team still happily married. Jake had adored Del's wife.

They squared up to each other, chest to chest and Jake got to his feet, prepared to intervene if necessary. Then Del laughed and shoved Si's shoulder. "Next time tell us. You know we don't give a shit."

He glanced over to Ruiz for confirmation, who just shrugged and mumbled, "I don't care who you wanna fuck, as long as it's not me."

Si smacked him on the back. "Dude, I'd never put my dick anywhere near you."

"What's wrong with *me*?" Ruiz looked offended.

Del snorted. "Do you want a list?"

"Where do we start?" Si gave Del a conspiratorial grin, breaking into laughter when Ruiz huffed.

Jake breathed freer at the easing of tension. It seemed none of the team had an issue serving with gays. Fuck it, why hadn't he and Mitch forced the issue before? All the time they'd spent leaving at separate times and pretending to have appointments or be meeting girlfriends. Then pretending to be roommates to save money. What a fucking pointless waste of time.

Howie returned with keys in his hand. He looked a little uncertain as he approached the group, but Si winked at Jake. "You better mind the bar." He walked out with Howie, his hand in the small of Howie's back. For his part, Howie looked shell-shocked and wary, as if he thought he might be the butt of some joke.

Del stared after them then he shook his head and looked at Jake. "I'll go find Mitch."

"I'll do it," Jake said. He needed to make his peace with Mitch, or they could get everyone killed.

Jake followed the route taken by Si and Howie, hoping to find Mitch. He squinted against the late morning sunshine, looking for the tall, solid leader of the team. Jake found him around the side of the building checking the windows.

"Christ, JT, sorry, Jake. One push and these windows will fall out." Mitch demonstrated and the window frame wobbled.

"Hey, careful." Jake leapt forward to hold onto his property.

Mitch snorted, but he stepped away and went to the next window. It obligingly wobbled as he grabbed it. "The whole place is a death trap."

Jake growled under his breath. "So the place needs some work. I wasn't expecting a psycho to turn up on my doorstep."

"How are we gonna keep you safe here?" Mitch demanded. "Riley only has to breathe on the building and it'll fall down."

"You've kept me safe in tighter conditions than this. Remember Rwanda?"

Heat flared in Mitch's eyes as he stared at Jake. Rwanda had been the moment they'd allowed themselves to acknowledge the spark between them was more than friendship. Mitch had saved Jake's life, pushing him down as a hostile was about to put a bullet in the back of his head. The second the hotel door closed behind them Mitch reamed Jake out for his inattention and, in the next moment, pulled Jake into his arms and kissed him, his mouth hard and demanding.

Mitch's face softened for an instant then he pulled himself up. "You've gotta take this seriously, Jake."

Jake huffed and folded his arms. "I *am* taking it seriously, but what the hell do you expect me to do?"

"Let me get you away from here."

"No." That was the only thing Jake was sure about. He wasn't running from his life a second time. "If Riley's coming for me then I face him on my terms."

"Then let me protect you. JT... Jake, please." Mitch's voice cracked and Jake saw the depth of the feeling in his eyes. "I can't do that if you're arguing with me all the time."

Jake took a deep breath. "I can stay here?" Mitch nodded, although he obviously wasn't pleased with the idea. "What do you want me to do?"

"You can get your ass inside. You're a sitting target out here. I'm gonna get Si, Del and Ruiz to secure all the points of entry. I hope Riley takes his own sweet time because it's gonna take all day to secure."

"We're not settling in for a siege," Jake pointed out as Mitch wobbled the frame again. "It's one man. Leave the goddamn window alone."

"It's Riley and you don't know if he's bringing anyone

else."

Jake thought about it for a moment then shook his head. "Riley was always a suspicious bastard. He wouldn't trust anyone else. Whatever he wants, he'll come by himself."

"Why're you so sure?"

"The only people he trusted were the team and that's because he had to. If Riley wants to talk to me, or kill me, he'll come alone."

Mitch nodded in agreement. "Yeah, I agree with you. Now get inside." He pointed to the back door, and Jake tried to pay attention because now was not the time to focus on Mitch's muscles under his tight shirt. Jake let himself be herded through the back into the bar. It was only going to be a couple of days then Riley would be caught and the team would go away. Jake tried not to think about how much he didn't like that idea.

Inside, Jake blinked at the sudden gloom. As his eyes adjusted, he saw Si and Howie hadn't returned. He wasn't sure how he felt about Si's interest in his business partner. Jake wasn't jealous but he was concerned that Si was playing with Howie's affection. Jake was deadly serious when he'd said that Howie wasn't like them. Howie was possibly the gentlest person he'd ever met, and Jake handled him accordingly. He didn't know if Si could understand, but he wasn't going to let anyone, not even a brother like Si, hurt Howie.

Mitch strode over to Del and Ruiz and started giving orders. The two men listened intently and, to Jake's surprise, looked at him as if for his agreement. He appreciated the concern and gave them a nod to confirm they could make the temporary alterations to his bar.

"I'll work on the inside while you deal with the outside frames." Jake wanted—needed—to do something.

Mitch looked over at him. "The moment we sight Riley I want you to get down to the basement with Howie. He's not going anywhere near you."

"No way." Jake's skin crawled at the thought of being hidden away while heck knows what happened overhead.

Mitch scowled at him. "Jake—"

"Dude, I am not going into the basement." Jake wasn't going to back down, no matter how hard Mitch glared at him.

"Jake—"

"I'm a trained operative, for Christ's sake. One of your best. You know that. You've told me enough times."

Mitch looked as if he was about to explode. "You were—when you were part of our team. Now you're just a…" He trailed off as Jake scowled at him.

"A what?" Jake snarled.

"A barman. You're a barman. You haven't kept up your training."

"You don't know that."

"Not the training we do, unless you make a habit of eliminating your customers," Mitch insisted. "Don't be a stubborn fool. You'll get yourself killed. You'll get us killed. Riley knows us, he knows our tactics and he knows *you*. He's gonna expect you to come out all guns blazing."

"And he's gonna be right," Jake said, "but that doesn't mean to say I'm going to be a liability. You think I've spent the last two years drinking beer?" He huffed at Mitch's silence. "I did the same training as I did every day we worked together. I'm as fit as I ever was. I'm not going down into the basement, Mitch."

"What are you going to do?"

"I'm going to kill the bastard!"

Mitch expelled a low slow breath. "You follow my instructions."

Jake gave a tight nod. "You're the boss."

"You'd better remember that, because if you endanger me or my team I'll slap you in handcuffs and throw you in the basement myself."

The kinky joke trembling on Jake's lips died as he suddenly remembered a moment—with handcuffs—from their past. The dark, heated look in Mitch's eyes told Jake the same image had flooded his mind, too.

"JT—" Mitch lifted his hand to stroke Jake's cheek.

"Jake."

Mitch shook his head. "You don't think of yourself as Jake."

"I do." It had taken a long time but he was finally Jake inside his head.

"So why didn't you call this place Jake's Bar, instead of J.T's?"

"Because ol' Jake down the road told me he had the name and if I wanted to open a new bar it had to have a different one, so I called it J.T's. Six months later Jake closed his bar and now spends his nights in here."

Mitch grinned at him. "Why not Howie's?"

Jake shrugged. "Howie didn't want his name on the bar. We co-own the place though."

"He's been a good friend to you."

"If it hadn't been for him...." Jake chewed on his bottom lip as he wondered how much to admit to Mitch.

"Yes?" As Jake still hesitated, Mitch slid his hand down Jake's arm, sending fire along Jake's nerves. "Tell me. Whatever it is I can take it."

"I was angry. I drank too much. Hell, I was drunk all the time. I scared people away 'cause I was an asshole. Howie was the only one who didn't run. I was an asshole to him too, but he stuck by me." Jake had once asked Howie why he hadn't walked away like everyone else had when he was drunk and lashing out. Howie hadn't given him a proper answer then and Jake was too chickenshit to question him further.

"I'd have stuck by you if you'd given me the chance," Mitch said, and Jake could hear the anger he was holding back.

"I know," Jake admitted, "but I was in a dark place, Mitch. I had no clue what I was doing. I just needed to get away, from all of you. Every time I looked at any of you I saw Sharon with Riley standing over her."

"You should have told me. We could've worked it out. You could've had therapy."

"I didn't need fucking therapy," Jake said through gritted teeth. "I needed to get away. It's all in the past now anyway. At least it was before you turned up."

"Thanks," Mitch said drily. "Nice to know we're welcome."

"You know what I mean."

Mitch turned to stare into Jake's eyes. "You don't miss us? Miss me?"

"I miss you every day." Jake saw that his honest answer eased the tension around Mitch's eyes. He owed him the unvarnished truth. "I miss our home. Even those noisy dogs of old man Farman's. Sometimes I thought being apart from you would tear me up. But staying would have killed me more. I was breaking into pieces, Mitch. I just couldn't tell anyone."

"Even me?" Mitch asked.

"Especially you."

Mitch got the truth, even if it hurt them both to hear the words out loud.

Si stuck his head around the door. "You two haven't killed

each other yet?"

"Not yet," Jake said. "Is Riley here?"

"No sign of the bastard. Del and Ruiz are keeping watch."

"If he's going to attack it'll be at night, probably before dawn," Mitch said.

Jake and Si nodded. That's what they would do and Riley was trained the same way.

"We'll set two hour watches throughout the day and night. You ought to send Howie home." Mitch looked at Jake, but Si interrupted.

"He's insisting that he stays. I told him to stay at home when we left the SUV there."

"He did spot Moose," Jake pointed out.

"Only because Moose was a fucking idiot," Mitch snapped. "I don't care what Howie wants. The second Riley is spotted he stays in the basement. He'll kill us all if he tries to help. Riley will make mincemeat of him."

"Agreed," Si said. "But if Riley lays a hand on my boy I'm gonna rip out his intestines."

Jake and Mitch looked at each other. They'd never seen Si this possessive over anyone before. It was kind of cute, in a Hannibal kind of way.

Si growled under his breath. "Shut up. I can hear you two thinking from over here."

Jake laughed at him. "You know you're never gonna live this down, don't you?"

"I don't want to," Si admitted. "I like Howie. Really like him."

"Does he know this?" Jake asked.

"Not yet. But he will."

Jake was still unsure about the idea of Si pursuing Howie. They were chalk and cheese.

Si caught sight of Jake's expression. "I won't hurt him."

"You'd better not." Jake stabbed a finger at Si's abdomen and made a hooking gesture. "Or it'll be your intestines in danger."

Mitch sighed. "Howie should run like hell while he's got the chance."

"Too late. He's mine now." Si leered at them. "I'll leave you two alone to do... whatever you were doing."

"I haven't missed you at all," Jake said.

"Sure you have." Si smirked again and, thankfully, vanished leaving Jake and Mitch staring at each other.

Jake rolled his eyes. "He's still a dick."

"You expected anything less?" Mitch snorted. "We better get back out there before Del takes a shine to Carl."

Jake burst out laughing. "Now if you'd said Ruiz I might have believed you."

Ruiz was notorious for his conquests, although as far as Jake knew most of them had boobs and legs up to their armpits. Mind you, Jake had thought Si was straight so what the hell did he know?

Mitch opened the door and gestured for Jake to go first. As Jake went through the door he was sure he felt the ghost of a hand over his ass. He inwardly cursed the fact that Mitch's touch still had the ability to affect him so much.

Back in the bar Carl gave Jake a hard stare. "You gonna do what the boss says?"

"*I'm* the boss." Jake huffed. "This is my bar."

Behind him Mitch gave a derisive snort. "He's still determined to get himself killed."

"It isn't me who's gonna die," Jake said grimly.

"Don't underestimate him," Mitch warned. "Riley was always a cunning bastard."

"I trained him, remember? He knows my moves; I know his. You think he wants to talk to me, convince me of his innocence? Well that's what you guys are going to do. Let him get to me."

"You've got to be fucking kidding me. Riley steps one foot on this property and we'll have him. He doesn't get anywhere you."

Jake shook his head. "No."

Mitch gave him a flat stare. "You don't get to decide this, Jake. This is my decision. My orders are to protect you, not facilitate a fucking conference. Riley's a convicted felon. He gets captured or he dies. Those are the only two options."

"And this is—"

"Your bar. Yeah yeah, I get that." Familiar impatience threaded Mitch's tone. "You forgot rule number 1."

Jake stared at him. "No fucking way. You're not pulling that shit on me."

"What's rule number 1?" Carl asked as Si snickered.

"Mitch's word is fucking law. There is no other fucking law except Mitch's. And if you fucking forget Mitch rules the goddamn world, you'll be cleaning the latrines for a fucking week, with a toothbrush."

Si and Jake said it together. Jake knew it word perfect. Rule number 1 had been seared into his psyche by hours of scrubbing the fucking latrines with a fucking toothbrush. Mitch was ruthless when it came to discipline. It didn't matter that they'd been lovers. Jake had received the same punishment as everyone else. In all fairness, Mitch had given himself the same punishment whenever he'd stepped out of line.

Carl nodded approvingly. "No wonder Jake runs a tight ship here. He's been well-trained."

Mitch turned to Jake. "Jake was one of the best."

The breath caught in Jake's throat at the naked pain in Mitch's eyes. "Mitch—"

"You wanna be part of this operation, you obey *me*." Mitch scowled at Jake. "Same goes for you, Carl."

Carl saluted him. "Yes, sir."

Jake huffed. "Fine. Rule number 1. But who do you think cleans the fucking latrines here anyway?"

"I do," Howie had kept quiet up to then. *Now he has to pipe up?* Howie just raised his eyebrow at Jake's glare.

"He breaks the rules, he'll be cleaning them for a month," Mitch assured Howie.

"Sounds good to me." Howie smirked at Jake's scowl.

"Same goes for you," Mitch said. "You're a civilian and you're not trained. If I tell you to get down I mean it."

Howie nodded. "Whatever you say."

"The same goes for any of the team, including Jake. You listen to them. They want to keep you safe."

"Is Riley really that dangerous?" Howie looked nervous.

"He's more than dangerous," Jake said. "He's one of us."

CHAPTER 5

The team sat around a large table. Mitch had set Carl and Doug on look out. Someone, probably Del, had sketched out a map of the bar with the position of all the doors and windows, not that there were many. The bar was long, but dark and cavernous. The feeling of being hidden away was something that had appealed to Jake when he'd initially considered buying it. They'd spent the last hour thrashing out a plan for keeping watch.

Mitch looked around the table, his expression serious. "As I said before, Riley's a cunning bastard. There is nothing he doesn't know about us and he will use that to his advantage. He knows all our strengths and weaknesses."

"You've got weaknesses?" Howie grinned at Jake. "From the way Jake talked about you, you were all supermen who bled steel and ate bad guys for breakfast.

Mitch shot Jake a faint smile. "Well, we do, but like everyone we've all got our weak spots. I tried to beat it out of them, but I was never successful."

"Weakness? I ain't got no weakness." Si puffed out his chest and ignored the derisive snorts from the rest of his team.

Mitch rolled his eyes. "You're too ruthless, Si. You're an animal when you get angry."

At Howie's look of alarm, Si shot a disgusted look at Mitch. "Don't scare the boy."

"Well, it's true, ain't it? As for the rest, Ruiz is impatient and Del can be slow to make a decision."

Del and Ruiz just shrugged. It was nothing they hadn't heard before.

"What about Jake?" Howie grinned at him.

"We had to remind him the bastards shoot back."

Jake knew he'd had a Pollyanna approach to operations in the past—before Sharon's murder.

"And you?" Howie asked again. "What's your weakness."

Mitch gave a faint smile and slid a sideways glance at Jake, who forced himself not to react. He knew it as well as Mitch did. Jake had always been his weakness. Anytime Jake had been in danger Mitch had been beside himself until he knew Jake was safe. The two of them had often had words about that. Words, kisses and harsh make-up sex.

Howie couldn't hold back his gutted look, but Si shifted his chair closer, indicating, not very subtly, that he was there for him. Jake saw the realization slowly dawn on Howie. The huge man with the shaved head and dark-blond stubble was there—for him. Howie glanced over and Jake nodded, silently acknowledging that Si was a good man. Howie blushed then turned to Si, a shy smile on his face.

Jake caught Mitch staring at him. "What?"

"Nothing."

There was never *nothing* with Mitch, but before Jake could question him further Carl and Doug walked in, wiping their foreheads with the backs of their hands.

"Dang, it's as hot as hell out there. It's Del and Ruiz's turn to broil." Doug headed to the bar. "Howie, can I get a bottle of water?"

Howie went behind the bar, stuck two bottles on the top and poured them into glasses half-filled with ice. Doug drank half of his, his throat working hard, before he remembered his manners and murmured his thanks.

Carl sighed with relief. "This is good. You've got to get out there, guys."

"I'll go back out with Si later," Doug said. "May as well make myself useful. Moose can go with Mitch after that."

Mitch looked annoyed at someone else trying to give orders but he held his tongue. Jake imagined he'd be having a quiet word with Doug out of their hearing.

Jake looked around. "Where *is* Moose?" He'd not noticed Moose wasn't in the bar. Fuck, he had to be more alert. He'd gotten sloppy. Maybe Mitch had a point.

"He's gone to the store to buy provisions," Carl said. "He used to be in the catering corps. He should be back soon. We're gonna rest in Jake's room. Call if you need us."

Carl vanished out the door with Doug on his heels as Jake turned on Howie. "Why did you let him go? You know what he's gonna feed us."

"It was Carl's fault," Howie protested. "I couldn't stop him."

"What's he going to feed us?" Mitch asked suspiciously.

"Sloppy Joes," Jake said.

"What's wrong with that? I like Sloppy Joes."

Jake snorted. "You've never tried Moose's cooking. He used to take over from me and Howie if we had a night off."

Mitch grinned at him. "Bad?"

"You have no idea."

"He nearly got us shut down our first year. Gave the customers food poisoning," Howie said.

"But Carl just told us Moose was in the catering corps when he was in the army."

"Carl didn't want to shop so he volunteered Moose. He was right, Moose *was* in the catering corps but they didn't let him near any food." Jake looked at Howie. "You've gotta cook with him."

Howie looked positively alarmed. "I can't take charge. You know what he's like. You remember last time?"

"You don't have to cook. You just have to stop him killing us with raw ground beef. I'll send Si with you," Jake said firmly. "He can help you manage Moose."

Jake wasn't sure if Howie looked grateful or even more alarmed at the idea of Si being in there, too. Probably a mixture of both. He was going to have to warn Si to take it easy with Howie.

Moose's ears must have been burning as he walked into the bar, both hands loaded with bags. "Everything we need for Sloppy Joes." He beamed at them.

Jake held back a groan. "Howie and Si are gonna help you."

"I don't need help. I've been making Sloppy Joes for years."

"Humor me," Jake said. "I'm jumpy today."

Moose looked partly mollified and let Howie and Si relieve him of the bags. The three of them vanished into the kitchen.

"Christ, who's in fucking charge here?" Mitch's temper finally exploded, his patience pushed too far. "Howie should be making the chow and Si needs to be out here, not acting as a kitchen maid and nanny to your wet rag of a barman."

Jake's back stiffened. "Firstly, Howie is a partner in my business, not a barman. Secondly, do I fucking want you here? No, I don't, so you can shut the fuck up. Third—"

If there was a third, Jake didn't get to it. Mitch shoved him against the office door and kissed him, his mouth forceful and demanding. Jake opened his mouth to tell him to back the fuck off, but all that did was gave Mitch the opportunity to slide his tongue in to explore Jake's mouth. Jake squeaked, the sound captured by Mitch. He didn't know what to do with his hands, in the end settling for resting them lightly on Mitch's hips. Mitch raked one hand through Jake's hair, tangling in his curls, and the other cupped his ass. Once he realized Jake wasn't trying to pull away, Mitch gentled, giving him a chance to share the kiss. Mitch let all his pent-up emotions into the kiss, and Jake did the same. It was more than a meeting of mouths, or Mitch trying to be dominant. The two men shared the frustrations and anger of two years apart. Jake didn't try to wrest control from Mitch, but he didn't stand there, passive under Mitch's anger. Neither of them were hard. Jake could feel Mitch pushed up against him. This wasn't about sex. This was communication in the best way they knew how.

Finally, Mitch pulled away, dragging in a shaky breath. "What the hell are you doing to me?"

Jake tried to speak, swallowed hard to get some saliva down his dry throat. "Fuck knows. Fuck knows."

"Lukas was right. I shouldn't have come. I'll call him and get someone else here by tonight. Maybe Ali Ossain. He's a good man."

Anger flooded Jake's veins and he dug his fingers into Mitch's hips. "Don't you fucking dare, Mitchelson."

Mitch furrowed his brow. "I thought you didn't want me here?"

"I didn't. I don't. But you're here now, and you're not palming me off onto Ossie just because you can't stand the heat. Are you that much of a coward?" Jake refused to let Mitch look away from his gaze.

"I'm no coward. I just thought you'd prefer it."

"You're talking fuckin' crap, Mitch."

Mitch let out an explosive breath. "What the fuck do you want then? One minute you're shoving me away, the next you're hanging onto me. It's like being on a carousel with you,

Tyler. I don't know what you want from me."

Mitch's words hit home. He had no fucking idea what he wanted either. The only thing he did know was that he didn't want Mitch to leave. He had to stop pushing him away. Aside from their personal issues, there was no one he trusted more to keep him alive when a psycho ex-team-mate/best friend/brother-in-law came calling. Not even Ossie whose reputation was legendary.

"I want you to get me through the next few days," Jake said. "As for after that, I have no idea, but I know I don't want you to go."

Mitch studied him carefully for a moment. "Fair enough. You and me can wait. Not forever, but long enough to get through this."

Jake nodded. "And you're in charge. We'll talk to the guys, especially Carl, Doug and Moose. Mitch's rule number 1."

Mitch grinned wickedly. "I've got three toothbrushes in my pack."

Jake gave him a sour look. "Why does that not surprise me? I'm gonna go into the kitchen and send Si out. He needs to be out here."

"'Kay. I need to talk to Lukas."

Mitch took a step back and Jake let his hands fall from Mitch's sides. From the heated stares they gave each other, they both regretted the distance between them. But Mitch dug out his phone and Jake headed into the kitchen.

Jake stopped inside the kitchen door and surveyed the scene. "I see you boys are busy."

Moose, Si and Howie looked up from the table where they were drinking ice tea.

Moose shook his head. "We've *been* busy. Now we've finished and Si is telling us all about your escapades together."

Jake glared at Si. "And you thought this was a good idea?"

Si gave him an unrepentant smirk. "Fair's fair. I remember you doing the same to me when I was going out with Chloe." Howie stiffened at the girl's name and he stared wide-eyed at Si, who reached over the table and grasped his hand. "I'm bisexual, okay?"

Jake was damned sure from the conversations he'd had with Howie that it wasn't okay at all, but Si didn't need to deal with Howie's hang-ups right this second. To Jake's surprise, Howie just took a breath and nodded. "It's okay."

Si beamed at Howie who smiled tentatively back.

Moose just shook his head. "Is it something they put in the water? You boys all being queer-like?" He didn't seem bothered, just resigned.

Si just clapped Moose on the back. "You ought to try it some time."

"No way, young fella. I only like—" Moose shaped the female form with his hands. Jake noticed said female had a rather large rack.

"Each to their own. I like both," Si said.

"Dick for me," Jake said quickly and Howie nodded in agreement.

Jake went to the fridge and poured himself a glass of tea. "Mitch wants you back out there, Si."

Si swallowed down the last of his drink and placed the glass in the dishwasher. "'Kay. If you need help, let me know." It was more than obvious he was only looking at Howie.

Jake took Si's place at the table. Moose tipped back his glass and did the same as Si. "I'll see what Mitch wants," he drawled, then ambled out of the kitchen, leaving Jake and Howie staring at each other.

"Howie—"

"He really likes me." Howie sounded as giddy as a girl on her first date.

"Si's a good man—"

"I won't hurt him, I promise."

Jake stared at him, shocked. "I never thought in a million years *you* would hurt *Si*."

Howie's lips quirked up at one side. "I've no idea why he likes me but he does."

"I think I might know," Jake said. "Not every man wants a fighter, Howie. Sometimes a man just wants to come home to a warm body and a warm heart." He didn't feel bad about quoting Si's own words.

"That's not what you want though, is it?" Howie asked shrewdly.

Jake shrugged. "Maybe I want a little of both."

"Is that what you had before? With Mitch?"

"I think sometimes we forgot the warm hearts. It was hard when we worked together every day, y'know? We'd come home tired and grouchy. Mitch was my boss at work and he'd forget he wasn't the boss at home. I got tired of jumping to attention when all I wanted was a cuddle." Jake's lips twitched as he admitted that he liked being cuddled.

"Did you ever tell him that?"

"I'm not so hot on the touchy-feely stuff. We'd get over it by fucking each other senseless rather than talking it out."

"Is that why it was so easy to walk away?"

Howie's casual comment hit home. Jake's fists clenched and he counted to ten rather than lash out. Howie didn't know—how could he— just how much that hurt.

Jake closed his eyes and then opened them. "It wasn't easy, Howie. You know that. You saw me after I left."

"You should've stayed and worked it out," Howie said

stubbornly. "You should have given Mitch the chance."

Howie looked over Jake's shoulder and Jake knew, without turning around, who was standing there. Jake wasn't surprised when Howie got to his feet and excused himself. Jake stayed where he was, staring down at his empty glass of tea.

Mitch went to the fridge, drew out the jug of tea and filled a glass for himself. He waved the jug at Jake who shook his head. Mitch sat in Howie's place and took a long swallow of the cold liquid before he spoke. "Howie's a literal guy."

"You noticed?" Jake huffed. "He's great but he sees everything in black and white."

"I understand why you left."

Jake tilted his head in surprise. "You do?"

Mitch leaned back in his chair and dropped his chin onto his black-clad chest. Jake noticed how tired he looked and remembered Si saying Mitch had spent all night watching him. "Understanding is not saying I forgive you. But you were falling apart and I didn't see that. I'm sorry."

Jake's fingers tightened around his glass. It hurt to know Mitch hadn't forgiven him, but what did he expect? "I should've told you."

"Yeah, you should've." Mitch sat up and took Jake's hand. "After we take Riley, you and me are gonna talk. Okay?"

Jake nodded and this time he didn't move his hand.

He wasn't sure how long they stayed like that, Mitch drinking his tea with one hand and holding Jake's with the other. But then Moose came in to check on the chow, with Howie following behind him. Moose was grumbling about Howie checking up on him and the peaceful moment they shared was lost. Mitch excused himself. Jake stayed at the table to act as referee. He had nothing better to do at that moment.

The loud bang close to them made the three of them jump. There was a brief pause, then another one and the glasses skittered across the table.

Howie turned startled eyes to Jake. "What the hell was that?"

"Fuck knows. It didn't sound like gunfire."

Moose nodded in agreement. "Ain't no weapon. Sounds more like a nailgun."

Jake left the kitchen in search of the noise. He found Ruiz and Carl shoring up the back windows with large sheets of plywood.

"What the hell are you doing?" he asked.

"Boss' orders," Ruiz said, hefting another sheet. "We're sealing all the windows."

Jake pressed his lips together and went in search of Mitch. He found him by the bar, talking to someone on his phone. "We need to talk."

Mitch raised a hand to stop him. Jake was about to tell him where to stick his orders when Mitch said, "Jake's here, Lukas. I'll put you on speaker." He placed the phone on the bar so they could both hear what the section leader had to say.

"I'm here," Jake confirmed.

"Good." Lukas' voice sounded tinny and clipped. "I received a call from a farm about a hundred and fifty klicks from you. They told me another truck was stolen last night. Someone spotted the driver and he matches Riley's description. We got a photo from the LEOs. I've sent it to Mitch."

"Why're you telling us this now? We know he's local," Jake said.

"Because Riley swapped vehicles this morning. He's now

driving a Hummer."

"Shit. If he wants he can just drive straight through the bar." Jake stepped back, catching the rail at the bottom of the bar. His ankle twisted and he would've fallen if Mitch hadn't caught him with one arm. "Fuck!"

"Are you okay?" Lukas barked, obviously concerned.

Jake breathed through the pain shooting up his shin and calf. "I'm fine. I just twisted my ankle."

"He's okay," Mitch rumbled, although he didn't let go of Jake. Instead, he steered him into a wooden chair and dropped to his knees to inspect Jake's foot.

"Now's not the time to do anything stupid," Lukas snapped.

Jake gritted his teeth. "Got that."

Mitch gently slid Jake's foot out of his boot and peeled off his sock. "Lukas, find that Hummer. We need to know where he is now."

"'kay, out." Lukas disconnected the call.

"At this rate he'll be driving down Main Street in five minutes," Jake pointed out to Mitch. He breathed steadily, hoping to minimize the pain, and was relieved to find it was better than he'd expected. The major problem was not the pain in his ankle but his body's reaction to the touch of Mitch's warm hands on his calf and ankle. His dick slowly filled as Mitch rotated his foot.

"Yeah. He's gonna be here today," Mitch agreed.

Breathe in, breathe out. Jake inhaled and exhaled slowly, trying to quell his boner with thoughts of anything except Mitch's hand on him.

"Your ankle looks okay. You should be able to walk on it." Mitch stayed where he was and eased the sock back over Jake's foot then slipped his boot on.

Jake couldn't let it go without making a comment. "I can

dress myself, dude."

Mitch rolled his eyes and got to his feet. "You're such an ungrateful bastard."

And right then Jake was taken to another moment when Mitch dressed him with exquisite tenderness; the day of Sharon's funeral, when Jake wouldn't have even gotten out of bed if it hadn't been for Mitch.

"Jake, what's the matter?" Mitch sounded alarmed.

Jake looked up at him, aware tears had spilled over on his cheeks. "Christ, how can you even talk to me?" His voice was raw and filled with pain.

"Jake?"

"What I did to you, after everything you did for me. How can you even bear to look at me again?"

Mitch wiped away the tears on Jake's cheek with his thumbs. "You were hurting."

Jake shook his head. "Walking away from you was unforgivable."

"You got all that from me checking your ankle?"

"Kinda."

Mitch cupped Jake's jaw and bent down to brush his lips with the lightest of kisses. "Your timing is shit, Jake. Can we take a rain check on the apologies until Riley is secured?"

"Yeah." Jake would rather have got the 'I'm a stupid dick' revelation over and done with, but Mitch was right, his timing was shit.

Jake stood up, gingerly testing his ankle. There was a slight twinge but nothing he couldn't live with.

"Can you walk?" Mitch asked.

"I can run a marathon," Jake assured him.

Mitch chuckled loudly. "Do that tomorrow. Today might be a bit busy."

CHAPTER 6

Jake was ready to punch something—or someone. He couldn't stand being cooped up in the bar like a fucking prisoner. Mitch refused to let him out to help with the barricades or the windows and Howie was doing an impromptu stock take with Moose's assistance. Once the windows had been boarded up inside, it left Jake with nothing to do except stare at the four walls. He refused to think of the paperwork he could be doing, he wasn't that desperate—except he was.

He cursed Riley for putting him in this position; trapped inside his own home with nothing to do except pour endless drinks for the men sent to protect him. That chapped his hide, too. This siege was affecting his bottom line. He'd fucking charge Riley for every drink he poured.

Del looked at him curiously when Jake shoved a large soda over to him so hard the liquid slopped over the side. "Something wrong?"

"Where do I start?" Jake exhaled loudly. "I'm trapped in my own home waiting for my sister's murderer to kill me, you lot are drinking my profits—"

"You're missing a great opportunity," Del said, before he slurped half the glass of soda.

"To do what?"

Del sat on one the bar stools as if he was going to make himself comfortable. "Do you think Riley would go to all this trouble just to kill you?"

Jake narrowed his eyes. “Go on.”

“You know Riley better than anyone. He was your best friend; someone you’ve known since grade school.”

“I thought I knew him,” Jake said, “right up until the moment he murdered my sister.”

Del carried on as if Jake hadn’t spoken. “Do you really think Riley would plan his escape from jail and travel four thousand klicks just to shoot you?”

“You obviously don’t.” Jake couldn’t see where Del was leading with this but he was curious as to why Del was giving Riley an out for his behavior. Del and Riley hadn’t been that close as Jake recalled. In fact, he remembered them clashing on more than one occasion.

Del wiped condensation from his glass and sucked his finger. He seemed to be choosing his words and Jake gave him time to think. He hadn’t worked with Del for as long as he had the rest of the team, but he trusted him implicitly.

“I think you should use this time to think about Riley’s motives.”

Jake didn’t give a shit about Riley’s motives. “He murdered my sister. I caught him in the act.”

Del shook his head. “You saw him standing over your sister holding the knife. You didn’t see him kill her. You told those cops...” He paused, obviously trying to remember their names.

Jake furrowed his brow and dragged their names out of his memory. “Sanchez and... Marshall? They were investigating burglaries in the area.”

“Yes. You told them you didn’t see him actually put the knife in her chest.” As Jake flinched, Del looked apologetic. “I’m sorry, my friend.”

“You seem very sure of his innocence.” Jake spat the words through gritted teeth.

“He always said he didn’t do it.” Del gazed at him, his eyes wide and steady.

“And you believe him.”

“The question is, my friend, why don’t *you*?” Del drank the last of the soda and placed the glass carefully on the bar. “Look, it doesn’t matter what I think. Riley doesn’t care about me. What matters is what you think. He cares about *you*. He’s gone to a lot of trouble to convince you he’s innocent. The least you could do is listen.”

Del got off the barstool and walked away without waiting for Jake’s response. Not that Jake knew what to say. He cleared away the glass then sat on the bar stool recently vacated by Del and stared at one of the old metal Coca-Cola signs on the walls.

“What the fuck?” he muttered.

“You talking to yourself now, dude?” Si grinned at him.

Jake had been so deep in thought he hadn’t heard Si come in. “What?”

“You’re talking to yourself. First sign of madness and all that.” When Jake didn’t respond, Si just shook his head. “Never mind. Can I have a bottle of water?”

“Help yourself,” Jake said absently.

“Okay.” Si drew out the word and looked justifiably surprised as Jake had yelled at Ruiz only an hour earlier when he tried to help himself to drinks. “Wanna tell me what’s got you so freaked out?”

“Del just said he thinks Riley didn’t kill Sharon and that I should listen to him when he gets his ass here.”

Si let out an explosive breath. “That again?”

Jake raised an eyebrow. “Again? You know about this?” When Si didn’t respond, he said, “Si? Did you know Del thought Riley was innocent?”

Si nodded with obvious reluctance. “Just ignore him.”

"Do *you* believe he was innocent? Does Ruiz? Does Mitch?"

"Wait, hold on. In order, no, I think the man's guilty and should fry. No and I don't know."

"Why didn't Del tell me?"

"Dude, you were a mess after Sharon's death. Do you remember what *anyone* said to you?"

Jake had to admit Si had a point. From the moment he caught Riley standing over Sharon's body, he couldn't remember a thing anyone said to him. Everything was muffled as though he'd been wrapped in layers and layers of cotton. "Do you think Del helped Riley to escape?"

Si gave him an exasperated look. "Don't be a fucking idiot."

"You think I'm an idiot? After you tell me this?"

"I didn't tell you. Del did," Si pointed out. "And you're an idiot if you think Del would do anything to jeopardize his career."

Another good point. Del was cautious to a fault.

Jake rubbed his temples. His head was starting to pound. "I don't know what to think any more."

"I think you should listen to Del and spend some time thinking about Riley. He's gonna be here soon and your reaction will be the key as to how it's gonna pan out."

"And here I thought Mitch was in charge."

Si didn't laugh at Jake's quip. "He may be the boss but he'll take his cue from you. Always has."

And that was the key to their relationship and the success of the team. Theirs had been a partnership, not a dictatorship. Apart from Rule 1.

Si wandered off leaving Jake alone once more to think. Needing somewhere quiet where he was unlikely to be disturbed, Jake grabbed a bottle of water and headed into the back of the building to his bedroom. He would've preferred to go outside and stare up at the stars, but he knew Mitch would explode if he stepped one foot out of the bar.

Jake tossed the pile of sleeping bags and mats that had been dumped on his bed onto the floor, propped a pillow against the headboard and laid on his bed, his boots resting on the comforter. His mom would've had a fit if she'd caught him with his boots on, but he didn't want to take them off in case he suddenly had to spring into action.

He was stunned by Del's sudden revelation and even more so by Del's suggestion that he ought to give Riley the fucking time of day when he turned up. "I'll give him a bullet between the eyes," he muttered. He closed his eyes and, for the first time in months, Jake deliberately thought about the moment his world had turned to hell.

Two Years Ago:

JT steered his truck onto the driveway of his sister's house. As usual he was going to watch the game with Riley while Sharon went shopping with friends. Riley had left a message to ask him to pick up more beer, so he was later than normal, but he'd be just in time for kick-off.

He hoped Riley had already ordered the pizzas because he was starving. He'd missed breakfast and lunch because he and Mitch had slept late and Mitch had fucked him until he'd had lost all sense of time. When he'd finally woken up he was already running late for his date with Riley. Mitch never joined them. He'd have rather had his eyes burned out of their sockets than watch a football game. JT had kissed him, picked up Riley's text and headed for the store.

JT screeched to a noisy halt in the drive, reminding himself yet again to check the tires, and grabbed the beer from the trunk. He jogged around the side of the house and entered the kitchen without knocking. "I'm here, dude. Hope you've got the pizza. Pepperoni, right?"

He rocked on his heels as the breath punched out of him. His brother-in-law, best friend and team mate turned to him, a bloody knife in his right hand. A crimson drop slid off the tip of the blade.

"JT, I..."

Riley's anguished whisper broke the binds that seemed to have JT frozen in place. He stepped forward and finally saw what Riley was standing over. Sharon lay on the floor, a large, red mass on the front of her shirt, her skirt rucked up around her waist. She wasn't moving, and she stared up at the ceiling, her eyes fixed and glazed. JT had seen that look too many times before not to recognize the mask of death.

"Christ! Sharon! Riley, what have you done?" JT chucked the beer onto the counter, uncaring at the loud crack from one of the bottles.

"I didn't do it, JT, I found her like this." As Riley spoke he waved the knife and another drop of blood joined the crimson mass beneath Sharon's body.

JT drew a gun on the man he called brother, and trained it at Riley's head. "Drop the knife."

Riley swallowed hard, his throat working as he said, "JT, you gotta believe me, I didn't do it. I love her."

"Drop the knife and lock your hands behind your head." Despite the rage and grief welling up inside JT he stayed where he was until Riley placed the knife on the counter top. "Where's your weapon?"

"Locked up. Both of them are," Riley said. "I found her like this, I swear."

JT ignored his desperate pleas, keeping the gun on Riley as he called 911. Neither man moved, even as the sirens got closer, until a uniformed officer relieved JT of his weapon while another handcuffed Riley.

One of the officers led him away from Sharon's body and, sometime later, Mitch arrived, barking orders at the annoyed police officers and holding JT in his arms, but he had no clue what happened to Riley.

Riley had denied it all, saying he'd found his wife dead after returning from collecting the pizzas, but he was convicted on JT's testimony, the fact that only his fingerprints were found on the murder weapon and one damning piece of circumstantial evidence, a large life insurance policy taken out against Sharon by Riley the previous month.

JT watched the jury find Riley guilty and walked out of the courtroom to hand in his resignation to Lukas.

"He was guilty. No question. Riley Ward murdered my sister," Jake told the empty room. He drew his legs up to his chest and wrapped his arms around them, hugging himself tight. He'd been so sure of Riley's guilt.

Riley hadn't been able to offer any other explanation. He hadn't seen anyone leave the house. Nor had the neighbors and many of them were willing to testify that Riley and Sharon had been having arguments. That was a shock to Jake. He'd had no clue there were problems in his sister's marriage. That hurt, too. The fact that neither of them had ever confided in him.

"Jake? Where the hell are you?" Mitch's increasingly irritated voice broke into Jake's musing.

"I'm in the bedroom," Jake called.

Mitch stood in the doorway, thunderclouds gathering above his knitted brows. "What the hell are you doing back here? You're not supposed to be on your own."

Jake swung his legs over the side of the bed. "I needed some time to think."

Mitch frowned. "You couldn't do that in the bar?"

"Do you think Riley's guilty?" Jake demanded.

Mitch opened his mouth and shut it again. "What kind of question is that?"

"One that deserves an honest answer. Do you think Riley murdered my sister?" Mitch took so long to respond that Jake realized he'd gotten his answer. "You don't. Fuck! You think he was innocent?"

"I don't know," Mitch said, "and that's the truth. I think the case against Riley was circumstantial."

"But I—"

"Didn't see Riley stick the knife in Sharon's chest." Mitch's face softened at Jake's flinch but he continued. "Anyone could've killed her and escaped. She always left the doors unlocked no matter how many times we told her not to."

Jake felt betrayed. "Si believes me. He thinks he's guilty."

"Si believes everyone is guilty until proven innocent. Usually after they've eaten a bullet. You, on the other hand, are willing to give people the benefit of the doubt. Why can't you this time?"

"He killed my sister!" Jake yelled.

"And that's why you can't think objectively about this case, Jake. He killed the one person you loved above everyone else." Jake was about to object but Mitch forestalled him. "Yes, even above me. I knew that and it was okay. I could deal with knowing you loved her more. She was your sister."

"What are you telling me? I sent an innocent man to jail?"

"Maybe," Mitch said bluntly. "And now he's coming to find you."

"To get his revenge."

Mitch sat on the edge of the bed, next to Jake, and reached for his hand. "I'm not about to let Riley Ward anywhere near you. I don't care if he wants to talk to you or kill you."

"Even though you believe he's innocent?"

"It doesn't matter what I think. He's an escaped convict." Mitch got to his feet. "And you aren't supposed to be on your own. You could still push your fist through any of the windows. Come on, back to the bar." Jake let Mitch draw him up and into his arms. "I won't let him hurt you, JT," Mitch whispered.

Jake buried his head in the crook of Mitch's neck. "Too late."

Mitch stroked Jake's hair. "I know, babe. I know."

Jake stayed where he was for a long time, resting against Mitch while he thought about his conversations with Del and Mitch. He still believed Riley was guilty. With every fiber of his being he believed Riley stabbed his sister, but perhaps he needed to process how he was going to deal with seeing Riley face to face.

Eventually Mitch sighed. "I could stay here like this forever, but I've got work to do."

"*You* have," Jake bitched. "All I'm doing is serving drinks."

"Well, this is a bar. Isn't that what you're supposed to do?"

Jake raised his head. "I don't mind serving drinks when I get paid for them," he said tartly. "You guys are drinking me out of house and home."

"Send the bill to Lukas. I'm sure he'd be happy to cough up."

Jake rapped his knuckles on Mitch's forehead. "Did you get dropped on your head recently?"

Mitch snickered. Lukas was notoriously tight-fisted. Jake could send him a invoice and Lukas would probably bill him for the team's services. He thought he'd try it anyway.

Si poked his head around the door. "You two stopped fucking?"

Mitch sighed. "What do you want?"

"Lukas is trying to get a hold of you. You're not answering your phone. He's pissed."

Jake frowned. Mitch never refused to answer his phone. It was a golden rule of being part of the team. Everyone had to be available twenty-four seven. "Where's your phone?"

Mitch patted his pockets. "Damn, I left it in the bar."

"Lukas is gonna string you up by your nuts," Si said. He held out Mitch's cell phone.

"He'd better get in line," Jake growled, snatching it from Si. "What the hell were you thinking, Mitch? You're never supposed to be out of contact. Never." He handed the phone to Mitch with another growl. "Call Lukas, now."

Si vanished with an annoyingly smug chuckle, leaving Jake to glare at Mitch.

"I'm sorry, I went looking for you. I didn't think about my phone."

"You're a fucking idiot, Mitch. Call him before he pops a vein."

Jake folded his arms and waited. Mitch's lips twitched but he pressed Lukas' number. Within a second Lukas answered. He wasn't on speaker but Jake could hear him as clearly as if he were. Lukas was loud and he was pissed off. From past experience Jake knew it was best to let their section leader shout until he'd got it off his chest.

"Where the hell were you? Where was your phone? You should have answered immediately! Herding fucking cats would be easier. Count yourself lucky I'm not booting you

out of the team..." And the one Jake had been waiting to hear... *"Rule number 1!"*

Mitch rolled his eyes at Jake, who gave him a wide-eyed innocent stare back. Mitch huffed, apologized, promised to send his first-born to Lukas and confirmed he had brought extra toothbrushes.

"Latrine duty?" Jake asked when Mitch slipped the phone in his pocket.

"Latrine duty," Mitch said. "Although I don't know why you're laughing. You broke rule number 1 too."

Jake bit his lip, so he had. By retreating to the bedroom to think. "Damn."

"Come on. Let's get it over with before Riley turns up."

Mitch rummaged around the pile of sleeping bags, mats and backpacks to find his own. He pulled out two toothbrushes and handed one to Jake.

Jake looked at the toothbrush. He'd hated latrine duty in the past. Now... Oh well, the bathrooms needed cleaning and he could think of worse things than scrubbing them in Mitch's company.

They walked back into the bar, intending to let someone know what they were doing. Si, Howie, Ruiz and Moose were sitting in one of the booths.

They all looked over as the two men walked in and Si grinned when he spied the toothbrushes. "Rule number 1?"

"Ya got it," Mitch said sourly.

"You got latrine duty too, JT... Jake?" Ruiz asked.

Jake nodded. "I broke the rules."

"Any excuse to get each other into the bathroom." Si chuckled, laughing ever louder when Mitch and Jake sent twin glares of disgust his way. "Go scrub. When you're done the Sloppy Joes will be ready."

"Would've been ready hours ago," Moose grumbled, "if

we hadn't been cooking by fucking committee."

Jake backed out of the bar, and Mitch followed him. Jake sensed a storm brewing. He'd let the boys deal with that one all by themselves.

CHAPTER 7

Jake pushed open the door to the restrooms and headed for the janitorial closet. “Men’s or women’s?”

“How many women do you get in here?” Mitch asked.

“One or two. It’s not the kind of place that attracts women.”

“We’ll do the men’s.”

“You’re the boss.”

Mitch grimaced and held up the toothbrush. “You’d think so, wouldn’t you? And yet here I am.”

Jake smirked at Mitch’s disgusted look. He handed him a bottle of cleaning spray and a pair of pink rubber gloves. “You broke your own rule, boss man. One for all and all for one and all that crap. Get scrubbing.”

It was strangely soothing scrubbing the tiles with a toothbrush, Mitch at his side doing the same thing. He’d cleaned worse places. If he was being honest this was probably the most thorough cleaning the bathroom had received in a long time. He just hoped it survived long enough for his customers to appreciate it. Not that they’d care. Jake had quickly learned that if his clients aimed for the urinals he was lucky.

Jake was mopping the floor when Del looked in. “Chow time.”

“Thank God for that,” Mitch said explosively.

Jake laughed. “You go on. I’ll put everything away.”

Mitch nodded and held his hand out for Jake’s

toothbrush. He had a ritual and although Jake rolled his eyes it was good to know some things hadn't changed in his absence.

By the time he'd arrived back in the bar Mitch was holding up the toothbrushes. Si and Ruiz looked resigned. Moose, Carl and Howie just looked confused.

"Gentlemen. Order has been restored in the universe. Justice has been seen to prevail. What is rule number 1?

"Mitch's word is fucking law. There is no other fucking law except Mitch's. And if you fucking forget Mitch rules the goddamn world, you'll be cleaning the latrines for a fucking week. With a toothbrush." Si, Ruiz and Jake cited the rule together.

"Exactly. And what do we do now?" Mitch waved the toothbrushes.

"Shove them where the sun don't shine."

"He means shove them in the trash," Jake supplied to non-team members who were looking alarmed.

He took the toothbrushes and threw them out. The point of the end ritual was to show the punishment was over. Mitch didn't bear grudges. Jake just hoped that applied to him too.

They ate in shifts. Jake ate with Mitch, Howie, Moose, Si and Carl. Del, Ruiz and Doug kept guard until Mitch, Moose and Si were finished. Then the men swapped over. Once more Jake found himself without something to do, other than clear up the kitchen. He didn't mind this work usually, it was part and parcel of running the bar, but under the circumstances Jake felt it was a waste of his talents.

Del helped him clear away the plates. Jake would have preferred almost anyone except Del after the conversation they'd had, which was probably the reason Mitch had assigned him to the task.

They worked in silence barring pleases and thank yous. Jake was stacking away the last plate when Del finally spoke.

"Are you pissed at me, Jake?"

Jake stiffened and turned to look at Del. "What do you think?"

"Have you spoken to Mitch?"

"About the fact he thinks the same as you?"

"Yeah."

Jake shook his head. "If you all thought he was innocent why didn't you say so at the time?"

Del pressed his lips together. "I did."

Jake's jaw would've hit the floor if it had been possible. "You did? When? I don't remember."

"Not to you. No one talked to you except Mitch. I talked to the team and the cops. The police and the D.A. weren't interested. They had an easy collar. No one was interested in finding Riley innocent."

"Especially me." Jake tried hard not to take it personally. He failed.

"Especially you," Del agreed, his tone somber.

Jake took in a breath and exhaled slowly. "I still think he killed Sharon. But say you're right, and he didn't do it, how does breaking out of jail prove anything?"

"It doesn't." Del looked frustrated. "It's a stupid idea. All he's liable to do is get himself killed."

"We agree on something at least."

Del dried his hands with a towel and handed it to Jake. "There's something else you need to know."

Jake waited, sure he wasn't going to like what he heard. "Go on."

"I kept in touch with Riley."

"You did what?"

"I told Lukas and Mitch. They gave their approval, as long

as they saw the communications and it didn't affect the team. Si and Ruiz don't know."

"How the hell could it not affect the team? You're corresponding with a convicted felon."

"One of us. Like you."

Jake just stared at Del, seeing the lines etched around his eyes and mouth. This misplaced loyalty was a strain the man had carried since the trial. "I thought I was important to you. I thought you liked Sharon. Doesn't she matter at all?"

"You left us, JT. You walked out and left us. I loved Sharon. We all did. My wife lost one of her best friends, think about that. You walked out but Riley got torn away from us. He was your best friend and he didn't kill his wife. I'll send someone else in here."

Del walked out leaving Jake frozen in the middle of the kitchen, the towel dangling from his hand.

Thirty seconds after Del left, Carl walked in, bearing a tray of glasses.

"More for the dishwasher, son." Carl studied Jake's face and placed the tray carefully on the countertop. "What's happened?"

Jake threw the towel into the corner of the room, not caring where it fell. Carl picked it up and hung it on the hook.

"Feeling better?" Carl asked.

"It's gonna take more than a towel to make me feel good," Jake growled.

"Do you wanna talk about it?" Knowing Carl, he'd prefer Jake to stick hot needles in his eyes than have a sharing-caring conversation.

Jake decided to spare him. "No, I'm fine."

Carl leaned back against the counter. "It's not easy when your old life comes a-knocking."

"You're telling me."

"Particularly when they want to tell you truths that aren't easy to hear."

Jake scowled at Carl. "Who's been talking?"

"Didn't need to, dumbass. You men were a team, a family. You had a bereavement and then a divorce. You're all hurting."

"Del thinks Riley is innocent. That he didn't kill my sister."

Carl nodded. "What do you think?"

"I saw him with my own two eyes." Jake stabbed at his eyes and clipped the corner of his right eye with his nail. "Ouch! Fuck!" It hurt like a bitch.

"You're gonna have one eye if you don't stop acting the fool. Here, let me look at it."

Carl tilted Jake's head to look at him. Jake's eye stung furiously and he couldn't stop it watering, but it didn't feel like any real damage had been done.

"What's going on?"

Jake heard the possessive growl in Mitch's voice. Blinking furiously, he turned to look at Mitch, who was scowling in the doorway. "I jabbed my finger in my eye."

"He'll live," Carl said, stepping away. "I'll leave you to it."

Mitch relaxed—a fraction—at Carl's departure. "Let me look." He came over but Jake batted his hands away.

"I'm fine," Jake said. "I'm going to wash out my eye and keep my hands below my waist."

"I want to look." Mitch manhandled Jake until he was close enough, and cupped Jake's jaw, tilting his head just as Carl had done.

"I'm fine," Jake grumbled but he subsided under Mitch's glare.

"It doesn't look like the cornea is scratched. I think you just scratched your eyelid." Mitch didn't seem in any hurry to let Jake go. "Are you all right?"

Jake knew he wasn't asking about his injury. He stepped away from Mitch, needing space between them before he had this conversation. "You should have told me. And if you tell me it's on a need to know basis, I'll stab your eyes out. I. Needed. To. Know."

Mitch shrugged. "It wasn't my call."

"Lukas?" Jake was going to have his ex-section leader's balls on toast.

"He gets to make those decisions."

Something in Mitch's tone made Jake look more closely at him, but Mitch's closely guarded expression didn't give anything away.

"Do you agree with him?" Jake demanded.

"We didn't know what we were gonna find until we got here, Jake. You haven't spoken to any of us since you left. It was the right call at the beginning."

"And now?"

"The cat's out of the bag. Del told you."

"He should get the toothbrush," Jake muttered.

Mitch pulled an empty toothbrush packet out of his pocket. "Already on it."

The restrooms were going to be the cleanest they'd been since Jake and Howie moved in.

Jake wiped away the last of his tears and glared at Mitch. "No more secrets, dude. You tell me what I need to know. You came in all guns blazing, swearing Riley would go back in a body bag, and now you're all 'poor fucking Riley'. You lied to me. Is this a protection or a retrieval operation?"

"We're protecting you. That's our primary mission. Lukas has given me full control on how we retrieve Riley."

"Did Del help Riley escape?"

Mitch shook his head. "Nothing to do with him or us."

Jake wasn't convinced. They could and had resources to pull off a jailbreak if they thought it necessary.

His skepticism must have shown on his face because Mitch caught both of his hands in his. "It wasn't us, Jake. This is Riley's move. If he hadn't escaped I'd never have found out where you were."

"I need to talk to Lukas."

Mitch transferred both of Jake's hands to his left and pulled out his phone.

"Yes?"

Jake heard the familiar greeting snap of his section leader.

"Lukas? Jake needs to talk to you." Mitch nodded at Jake. He didn't seem in any hurry to let go of Jake's hands.

"Go ahead, Jake."

Jake took a deep breath. "You pull another fucking stunt like this and I'll have your balls for wind chimes. Do you understand? You don't turn my fucking life upside down and not give me full intel. I'm not a mark or a vic. You tell me everything, and I mean everything, or you're out of here and I'll take my chances with Riley fucking Ward on my own." He dragged in another breath.

There was a long pause before Lukas replied, then he said, "Have you finished?"

Jake grunted. "It depends on what you say next."

"You know I'm never going to give you the full intel. It's your job to obey orders, not question them."

Jake opened his mouth to explode but Mitch got there first. "You're not helping, Lukas."

"It's not my job to be fucking helpful," Lukas snapped impatiently. "It's my job to get it done. The "it" in this instance being to protect you and retrieve Ward. That's all you needed to know."

"Do you think he's innocent?" Jake demanded, furious again.

"I think there are questions unanswered from the original investigation." Lukas sounded cautious as if he was tripping his way through a potential minefield.

"So you do think he's innocent."

"That's not what I said and you know it."

"Lukas, have you got any more intel on Riley's whereabouts?" Mitch asked.

"He's changed vehicle again. About a hundred klicks now. This time an old Chevy."

Mitch frowned. "That's new. Why would he downgrade?"

"He'll know we'll be looking for the Hummer."

"He's gonna be here in a few hours."

"What's the time now?"

Mitch looked at his watch. "23:15." The team always used Zulu time in communication with Lukas.

"Contact me the second he arrives," Lukas ordered.

"You'll be the last to know," Jake assured him.

Lukas snorted. "I suppose you think I deserve that?"

Jake grinned at Mitch, unseen by Lukas. "Yes, yes I do."

"Go away, funny man. Make sure the team is ready, Mitch. And remember your orders."

"What orders?" Jake asked, but all he heard was the click as Lukas disconnected the call. He turned on Mitch. "What orders?"

"They're *my* orders," Mitch said. "Mine. Team leader, remember?"

Jake growled but he knew Mitch was right. He had no business knowing Lukas' orders. "Another fucking way to keep secrets."

"You know virtually everything, Jake."

"You said that before and look what crawled out of the

woodwork."

"I want you to think about the moment you saw Riley standing over Sharon. What was his expression?"

Jake thought back to that moment, the split second before he saw his sister on the floor. He pictured Riley's face in his mind. "He looked... shocked."

"Good, what else?"

"Just that. Shocked. Like he didn't expect me to walk in at that moment."

"But he knew you were coming to watch the game. You were the one person he should have been expecting. If he planned to kill Sharon, why didn't he let you find her? Why did he kill her then?"

"I asked myself that before, but I thought it was just an impulsive act. They'd had a fight or something and he'd snapped."

"You know Riley. Do you think he's the snapping type?"

Jake hadn't thought Riley capable of murdering his wife. Riley had killed people. They all had. The team's objective wasn't to eat donuts and guide old ladies across the road. But they'd killed on Lukas' orders and only when necessary. Still, the number of marks added up even though they didn't kill in anger. Did cold-blooded killing make it better? A justified death? The prosecution had argued that Riley hadn't snapped, he hadn't lost his temper. On the contrary, the insurance policy proved he had planned the act all the way along. They were short of money, and Jake had to admit Sharon liked spending it. A large injection of cash would've solved Riley's financial problems.

"Jake?"

Jake realized he'd not answered Mitch's question. "No, I don't think he was the type to snap. If anything, Riley planned and over-planned down to the minutest detail."

"Yes, he did," Mitch agreed. "He was an asset to the team because of his logistical skills."

"I was late because he asked me to pick up beer. He changed the schedule."

"Would that have been normal for Riley?"

Jake shook his head. "He hated unexpected events. But why was he holding the knife?"

Mitch thought for a moment. "If it had been me lying on the floor, with a knife in my chest, what's the first thing you would've done?"

"If I hadn't been thinking? Take it out. But I'm trained never to disturb anything, so as Riley."

"It was his wife. He loved her. Whatever troubles they were having you know how much Riley loved Sharon"

"So, you're saying Riley wasn't thinking because he was in shock. And that look on his face was genuine?"

"I'm saying it's one possibility, Jake. You were in shock, too. You both may have missed something."

"Like what?"

"Like someone sneaking out the back of the house?"

"They would have been covered in blood," Jake objected. "Riley was covered in blood, but CSU didn't find blood anywhere else in the house. And they did check. They did their job."

"I know they did." Mitch ran his hand through his hair. It was too short to ruffle much, but Jake itched to put back the stray hair. "I haven't got all the answers yet."

"Fuck." Jake collapsed into one of the kitchen chairs. It rocked under his weight.

"I know this is difficult for you."

"You have no fucking idea, Mitch."

Mitch stroked Jake's hair, an oddly paternal gesture. "Yeah, I do. I was screwed up too, Jake. By Sharon's murder, by Riley's betrayal, by you walking out. I never considered Riley was innocent either. It's taken two years of hard talking by Del to get me to even consider it, then Riley does this. This isn't easy for me or any of the team. Si thinks we're wrong. He and Del are barely speaking to each other."

Jake leaned into Mitch's touch. "I need to think. But keeping me locked up in here is sending me loco. Let me stand guard. If Riley is innocent, he wants to talk, not shoot."

Mitch shook his head. "Nice try but no dice. You can't leave the building. It'll be all over soon. Just a little longer. If I see you step one foot outside you'll be scrubbing the whole building with your own toothbrush."

Jake huffed but he knew Mitch wasn't going to change his mind. He was locked up in the bar until Riley made an appearance. Jake was tempted to offer the dude the keys to his truck if it would get him here quicker.

CHAPTER 8

Back in the bar, there was an air of tense excitement among the few occupants as if they knew things were about to happen. Jake had always felt the same before an operation; knowing everything was ready and anxious to start. This was the first time he hadn't felt that shared excitement. He wasn't a team member. He wasn't even the mark. He was the victim. Christ, he was having a pity party. Jake mentally shook the thought away. He needed to get the fuck over himself. Del and Ruiz were nowhere to be seen. Del was presumably still on punishment duty and Ruiz was on guard.

He wandered over to Howie and Si who were having a private party in one of the booths. Si raised his eyebrows as Jake approached. "I hear you have plans for our glorious section leader's balls."

Jake sighed. "Too much crap flung at me at once. You know I hate being out of the loop."

"I told them they should've told you first. Especially all the bullshit about Riley being innocent."

Jake studied Si's face. "You don't believe a word of it, do you?"

Si shook his head. "It's all horseshit."

"You think he's guilty."

"As the day he was born."

Jake knew that Si and Riley had clashed in the past, but he thought that was just the difference in their styles. They were like chalk and cheese. The careful Riley and the impetuous Si. Jake had ignored them when they butted heads except to tell them to cool it if they got too disruptive. The team were all different in their personalities, but when it counted, they'd all gelled together. Or so he'd thought.

"*Why* do you think he's guilty?"

"Sharon talked to Maria just before. She said she feared his temper."

Jake frowned. He never remembered Riley having a temper. "That doesn't sound like Riley."

Si shrugged. "Who knows what goes on behind closed doors?"

Jake thought of some of the things that went on behind his closed door with Mitch. He shook his head, trying to clear his thoughts. "What did she tell Maria?"

"She said they had financial problems. Riley was trying to fix it. She thought Riley was doing things behind her back but she wasn't sure what."

"That doesn't sound like Riley either." Jake bit on his thumbnail. "If Sharon wasn't my sister I'd say she was the one in deep shit and trying to pass the blame on Riley."

"You don't think she was capable of it?" Howie spoke for the first time.

"I don't know," Jake said honestly. "I'd never have thought so but my faith in my own judgment has taken a knock."

Si looked dubious. "Perhaps you ought to talk to some of her friends."

"I don't know who they were, aside from the team. We were a close-knit group. You know that better than most."

"Yeah, I do. We didn't have friends outside the team. "

"Maybe that was our problem. We were so tight that we were blind to the issues of our team mates." Jake shook his head. "She was my sister. She would've told me."

Si huffed. "Dude, I know you don't like women, but seriously, you can't be that blind."

Jake stared at him, uncomprehending. "What do you mean?"

"Sharon wouldn't have talked to you about her marital problems. Riley was your best friend and team mate. You're the very last person she would have gone to. Sharon talked to other women."

"Like Del's wife."

Si inclined his head in agreement. "Maria told Sharon to talk to you, but I guess she felt she couldn't betray Riley's confidence."

Jake felt gutted that his little sister felt she couldn't talk to him. They'd always been close and, when she fell in love with his best friend, it seemed serendipitous. Mitch had told him about that word. Meant to be. Everything had seemed to fall into place. Riley and Sharon, JT and Mitch. Christ, he'd been so naïve to think it would last forever.

"Sharon loved you, Jake. She thought the world of her older brother. Don't think badly of her for not talking to you."

"I loved her, too. I just wish she'd spoken to me first. I could've helped, maybe prevented Riley attacking her."

"If he did," Si said.

Jake frowned. "Don't you start with that crap! I thought you believed he was guilty."

"I do." Si ran a hand over his head. "I just know the others don't. You're gonna have to deal with that—before Riley turns up on your doorstep."

"If I'd known this was a welcome Riley back to the party op, I'd have thrown you out before you dug your heels in under my table," Jake said sourly.

"You know you're just weeping with excitement at seeing

us again."

Jake shoved at Si's shoulder. "Where the fuck did you get that stupid idea?"

"From me," Howie said.

"What?" Jake stared at him.

Howie shrugged. "You're different since they arrived."

"They told me my sister's murderer is free. Of course I'm different."

Howie shook his head. "It's not that. You seem more alive. As though you were just going through the motions before, but now your eyes are open and you're excited. You were born for this work."

Well, yeah, he was, but Jake also knew he couldn't keep on reliving the glory days. He listened to Carl and Doug rehash their lives in the military on a daily basis. He didn't want to be like that. He was proud of what he'd done, but he also knew that time was over.

Then Jake heard the squawk of a walkie-talkie.

"Hostile is here. Repeat. Hostile is here." Doug's voice was tinny. "Approaching the back in a truck. He hasn't seen us yet. Do we allow him to gain access?"

"Affirmative," Mitch replied. "Stay out of sight. Let him approach the back door. Si and I will greet him."

"Understood."

Jake looked over to find Mitch's attention focused on him. This was it. Riley was here.

Mitch barked out orders. "Si, secure Howie and Jake. Del and Ruiz, hold the doors to the basement. Carl and Moose, hold the front doors. Doug, keep your weapon trained on Riley. Si and I will guard the back. Do not let him get near Jake. Repeat. He doesn't get within ten feet of Jake. Radio silence from everyone except Doug until he's in the building."

Si looked at Howie. "Babe, go into the basement and don't

come out until I tell you."

Howie gave one nod and slid out of the booth, heading for the trapdoor behind the bar.

Si glared at Jake. "You do what Mitch tells you. Okay?"

As if on cue, Mitch ran over. "Behind the bar, Jake. Now!" Jake wanted to argue but he allowed Mitch to manhandle him over to the bar. "Stay there and keep your head down!"

Jake pulled out his weapon and waited. He was good at that.

"Hostile has parked the vehicle in the trees half a mile away. Still inside," Doug said. Silent minutes went by before he spoke again. "Hostile has exited the vehicle and is reconnoitering the area."

Jake and the team didn't need a play by play of what Riley was doing. It's what they'd all do. Riley was on unknown territory. He'd take his time and he'd be expecting trouble. Riley wasn't stupid enough to think Lukas wouldn't send at least one team to support Jake. Jake wondered if Riley knew Lukas would send his old team for a meet and greet. Then he mentally slapped himself. Of course he would know.

"Hostile is heading for the back of the bar. Repeat, back of the bar."

"Can you see a weapon?" Mitch asked.

"Negative."

"Riley wouldn't be stupid enough to come here without packing," Si said. "He must know Jake would shoot him first and ask questions later."

"What makes you assume I'm gonna bother asking any questions?" Jake muttered.

Si smirked. "Fair enough."

"Quiet." Mitch scowled at them. "I'm trying to listen to Doug."

Jake and Si obediently hushed and Mitch said, "Say that

again, Doug."

"Hostile has reached the sheds at the back. He's on the far side. He's...." There was a long pause, too long, before Doug said. "Hostile has a weapon. Can't see what it is but there's definitely something in his hand."

"Did everyone get that?" Mitch asked.

Jake heard the quiet slew of affirmatives. He let out a deep breath. Riley was here. In a moment they would be face to face and he would get justice.

"Jake? Jake?"

Jake looked over at Mitch. "Yeah?"

Mitch stared at him with a worried expression. "Are you gonna be okay?"

"I'll be fine. Just want to get it over with, y'know?"

Mitch nodded. "Stay behind the bar."

Jake rolled his eyes. "Yeah—"

He stopped as a crack thudded into the back wall, followed by two more. They were unmistakably bullets embedding in the wall of his bar.

"What the fuck?" Mitch bellowed. "Who the hell is firing? Doug?"

"Can't see the shooter. Someone is firing at hostile one."

Jake and Mitch exchanged startled glances. Who the hell was shooting at Riley?

"Is he hit?"

"Not yet." Doug's tone suggested it wouldn't be long before that situation changed.

"Is he close to the door?" Mitch asked.

"Five feet away. He's down. Hostile one is down."

Mitch nodded at Si and they wrenched open the back door. Jake held his breath as Mitch and Si rushed out, dragging Riley in with one hand each scooped under his armpits. Si slammed the door shut just as another slew of bullets thudded into the wood. Mitch pushed Riley to the floor while Si relieved him of his gun, handing it to Jake.

"Doug, can you see which direction the shooter is?" Mitch asked

The radio crackled into life. "Negative. The buildings are masking my view."

"Get back here now and keep your head down. Carl, Moose, get inside. You're sitting targets now. Guys, we have a new hostile outside. Do you copy?"

"Copy that," Carl said.

"Understood," Del said. "Is it safe to bring Howie into the bar?"

"Not yet. Keep him down there until hostile two has been neutralized. Riley is secured." Mitch hunkered down next to Riley. "Where're you hit?"

Riley grimaced. "Hit my thigh. Nowhere serious."

Mitch obviously agreed with his diagnosis because he looked over Riley to Si. "Cuff him," he ordered.

The rain of bullets had ceased, presumably because Riley was inside. Jake realized he'd been holding his breath, waiting for the hostile's next move. Without knowing who was out there, the team were going to be working in the dark.

Their first problem was being shackled to an old cast iron ring attached to one wall. Jake stood in the shelter of the bar, out of Riley's line of sight. He wanted to study him, to get his emotions under control before he had to face him. Unsurprisingly, prison had left its mark on the man, in the deep lines scored around his eyes, a shocking weight loss, and what hair he had left was almost gray now. Riley was the same age as Jake, but he could have been a decade older. He had a dark bruise on his left cheek; maybe a result of the accident. Riley tested his shackles, then subsided, presumably deciding he couldn't escape. Then he looked around, assessing his situation until he spotted Jake. His expression changed, became something pleading. Jake ignored him.

Once Riley was cuffed, Mitch resumed the questions. “Who’s shooting at you?”

Riley looked surprised, then wary. “I thought it was one of the team.”

“It wasn’t us.”

Riley looked over at Jake. “JT?”

Jake wanted to put a bullet in the murdering bastard’s head. He wasn’t taking his eyes off Riley until the killer was in a body bag, but he didn’t have to hold a conversation with him. Mitch stepped in front of Jake, deliberately breaking his line of sight.

“Am I going to need to take *your* weapon, too?” Mitch took Riley’s gun from Jake’s lax hands, tucking it in the back of his waistband.

Jake scowled at Mitch. “Try it and see what happens next.”

“You cause any trouble and I’ll shackle you next to him.” Mitch’s tone left no doubt he was deadly serious.

“You’ve got other things to worry about than me. Who the hell is after him?” Jake stabbed a finger at Riley.

“I don’t know. Jake, where’s your first aid kit?”

Jake pulled a zipped pouch from under the bar. “Here. What do you need it for?”

“You check Riley’s wound. I’m gonna call Lukas.”

“You’ve got to be joking?” Jake wasn’t going near Riley except to stick a bullet in him. He certainly wasn’t going to patch him up.

“Do I look like I’m fucking joking?” Mitch growled. “He’s not bleeding to death on my watch.”

“I’ll do it,” Si said. “Jake, guard the door.” Mitch looked

as if he was about to explode but Si cut him off. "For fuck's sake, Mitch, what do you expect? Gimme a toothbrush and I'll scrub the whole fucking bar if I have to but Jake stays away from Riley."

"I don't fucking bite," Riley grumbled.

They all ignored him.

Jake mouthed a thank you to Si and took his place at the door. He kept out of sight of the small window that remained. He didn't know if hostile two was a pro or just someone with a beef against Riley, but any shadow in the window made him a potential target.

"I'll call Lukas," Mitch said. "If we're under attack—again—I want to know why." He walked away leaving Jake and Si kneeling by Riley.

Si looked Riley in the eyes. "I'm going to look at your leg. Give me any reason to shoot you, fucker, and I'll do it."

Riley's lip curled. "Still a thug, Si? Nothing's changed. If you're gonna do it, just get on with it. If there is someone after me, I don't want to be caught with my pants down."

Si frowned as he inspected Riley's leg. "We need to get the bullet out." He ripped open the pants leg to get more access. "Hope you're not attached to these pants."

Riley did an awkward shrug. "I'm not. Can't speak for the dude who owned them a couple of hours ago."

"You stole them?" Si sneered as if it was nothing more than he expected.

"I liberated them from a clothes line. They probably haven't even noticed yet." Riley winced as Si poked at the wound with a pair of tweezers. "What about a shot of tequila to numb the pain?"

"You'll get nothing from my bar," Jake said flatly.

"You're not fucking drinking with someone shooting at you." Si dug deep in the wound and Jake took grim satisfaction in Riley's wince of pain.

"Ow! Fuck!"

"Stay the fuck still, Riley." Si snapped out his order. "You've had worse."

And then there was an awkward moment, because Riley had been shot before and Si had been the one to pick out the bullet. Only then Riley had been a friend and part of the team.

Jake turned back to the window and frowned. "Mitch, get over here."

Mitch jogged over to him. "What?"

"There's a vehicle near the trees. Can you see what it is?" Jake moved so that Mitch could take his place.

Mitch hummed. "It's too dark to see properly. Truck of some kind?"

"Yeah. I don't recognize it."

"Del, get up here." Mitch yelled down the stairs to the basement.

Jake heard heavy footsteps thumping up the stairs then Del appeared.

"Boss?"

"Keep eyes on the truck at one o'clock," Mitch ordered.

Del nodded and took his place.

Mitch nodded at Jake. "Come with me." He led Jake into the main bar. Jake was relieved to be away from Riley. Just looking at him made his stomach churn. Mitch pulled Jake into a light hold. "How're you doing?"

"I'm confused. Sick. Tired." Jake leaned against Mitch for a moment.

"Me too. But you know what this could mean, don't you?"

"I don't know anything." Jake's whole fucking world was upside down. There were too many questions and no answers worth a damn.

“We’re gonna find out, I promise.”

“If Riley didn’t murder Sharon….”

Mitch cupped Jake’s jaw and tilted his head, forcing Jake to meet his gaze. “Can you deal with that?”

Jake wrapped his hands around Mitch’s wrists. “That I sent an innocent man to jail? I don’t know, but now’s not the fucking time for me to have a meltdown over it. Someone else is trying to kill Riley, and us. We’ll catch them first then I’ll deal.”

Mitch brushed Jake’s lips. “You don’t have to do it by yourself.”

Amid not knowing what the fuck was going on, Mitch being by Jake’s side was something Jake was hanging onto

CHAPTER 9

"Mitch? Come in? Where's Moose and Carl?" Doug sounded over the radio.

"I don't know. I called them in." Mitch grabbed his walkie-talkie. "Moose? Carl? Come in?"

Neither of them replied. Mitch called again but there was still the same static emptiness.

Jake saw the worry on Mitch's face. "We need to get out there."

"Doug, we're going to check. Stay where you are. Del, take Si and check the front for the boys. Don't get in sight of the truck."

Del nodded. "Will do."

Before he could move there was a knock at the door. Jake and Mitch looked at each other. Mitch motioned to Jake.

Jake nodded and called out, "Who is it?"

"It's Moose. Can I come in?"

Mitch and Jake looked at each other. The door was unlocked and Moose knew it. Mitch indicated to Del to get behind the door and Si to get into position then he nodded to Jake.

"Hold on," Jake called out. Mitch went to the door and rattled the bolts as if he was unlocking the door.

Then he opened it, getting out of the way.

Moose was framed in the doorway, his eyes wide and his hands held high. He blinked rapidly and Jake nodded.

"Come in, Moose." Jake made his voice as cheerful as he

could.

"Whoever's behind the door, show yourself." A voice Jake didn't recognize barked out the order.

Del stayed where he was but Mitch moved into sight, his hands held up like Moose. "I'm here."

As they came into the bar, Jake saw the figure of a man behind Moose. From the tension in Moose's shoulders, Jake knew he had a weapon of some sort in his back.

"You all right, Moose?" Mitch asked, his voice calm and controlled.

Moose nodded tightly. "Yeah."

"What about Carl?"

"He got jumped. He's unconscious but he's alive."

"Stop talking," the stranger barked.

Moose gasped and coughed. "Quit jabbing that thing in my ribs."

"You don't need to hurt him," Mitch said. "What do you want?"

For the first time, Jake got a good look at the man. Something about his raggedly trimmed strawberry-blond hair and dark-rimmed glasses stirred a distant memory. "Who are you?"

"His name's Marshall," Moose said. "He's one of the new deputies."

"You're a police officer?" Mitch looked as confused as Jake felt. If this was police business why the hell did he attack Carl and Moose?

Marshall ignored Mitch and stared at Jake. "Hand over Riley Ward and I'll leave you alone."

In one smooth move, so Marshall didn't see, Jake closed his fingers around his gun and slid it into the back of his waistband. "What do you want with Riley? Did you help him escape?"

Marshall barked out a harsh laugh. "You're joking, right?"

"Then you were the one shooting at him?"

"I was trying to recapture him."

"By shooting him?" Jake said flatly.

Beads of sweat ran down Marshall's temples and Jake wasn't sure if the man was on a drug high. "He's worth the same dead or alive. Now hand him over or I'll arrest you all for aiding a convicted felon."

"Why hurt Carl and Moose?" Ignoring Mitch's annoyed growl, Jake moved from behind the bar. He wanted the stranger's attention focused on him. "If you're on police business, let go of Moose and we'll call the sheriff."

Marshall snarled at him. "Move one step closer and your friend is dead."

There were at least two guns trained on Marshall, but Jake didn't bother to inform him of that. "You can take Riley, Deputy Marshall. Come this way. He's in the back."

"Bring him here," Marshall ordered.

"You shot him in the leg."

"I don't care if he has to hop. Bring him here."

Jake looked at Mitch, who gave a brief nod. "Mitch will get Riley."

Mitch backed away around the bar and out of sight. Jake heard what sounded like Riley being uncuffed but he didn't appear immediately.

"Hurry the fuck up," Marshall said. "And don't think of making a run out the back or I put a bullet in your friend."

Jake heard footsteps and then Mitch reappeared, one hand around Riley's upper arm, with Riley leaning against him as he limped into the bar. Riley's eyes widened as he saw Marshall and said, "You?"

Mitch stared down at him. "You know him?"

"Yeah. He's one of the cops who arrested me at the scene."

Jake stiffened and stared at Marshall, trying to remember him but most of it was a haze. "You sure?"

"You think I'm gonna forget that?" Riley stared at Marshall with active dislike. "They worked me over in the cells and let their cop buddies know it was open season on the wife-killer."

Jake vaguely remembered one of the team telling him at the arraignment that Riley looked as if he'd been beaten up, but no one was caring much at that point.

"Get over here," Marshall said.

"Why're you here?" Jake said. "I don't understand why you're here."

"Don't you get it?" Marshall snarled.

Jake shook his head.

"She wasn't supposed to be there! The house was supposed to be empty. Sanchez said she was shopping."

"Who wasn't?" Jake's gut tightened as he realized what the man was saying. Everyone in the room froze. "Sharon?" he ground out. "*You* killed Sharon?"

"The stupid bitch threatened us. Said we'd be dead the second her husband heard about it."

An animalistic howl of pain filled the room and Jake turned to see Mitch, his arms tightly banded around Riley who struggled to get away.

"I'm gonna kill you!" Riley howled again. "You're a dead man, Marshall! A fucking dead man!"

"But why confess?" Jake said. "Why come here at all?"

"I'm finished. Sanchez got caught and is spilling his guts to the cops. If we go to prison and he," Marshall pointed at Riley, "gets to hear about it, we're dead."

"So, you heard about the escape and thought you'd kill him first?" Jake blinked. "That's fucking stupid."

Jake wasn't sure who moved first, but Riley threw his

head back and cracked Mitch on the nose. Mitch yelled and Riley took the opportunity to pull free, just as Marshall shoved Moose forward. There was a deafening crack, Moose stumbled and fell heavily to his knees. Jake saw the spreading red stain on the back of his shirt.

Marshall aimed at Jake, but Riley grabbed Mitch's gun and shot him. Marshall stumbled but fired at Riley. His aim was off and thudded into the wall opposite.

Jake shot Marshall again, but the fucker still didn't stop, trying to raise his gun one more time. Then he was flung forward, falling over Moose and landing on his back. Jake's ears rang with the discharge of the shotgun.

"Nobody shoots my friend, asswipe." Doug stood in the doorway, a satisfied look on his face.

CHAPTER 10

Determined Marshall would never get up again, Jake got to his feet and wiped the sweat from his brow. Adrenaline still pounded through his veins. It was almost a shame Marshall hadn't made any attempt to move, Jake needed the release. Just one twitch would be enough. Jake took aim at Marshall, not even lowering it when Mitch said, "The dude isn't getting up, Jake."

"You sure about that?" Riley said. He stood over Marshall's body, his hair plastered to his head as sweat trickled down his temples. "'Cause I swear the fucker just twitched."

Marshall's breath was little more than a rattle in his throat as his hands pressed to the wounds in his chest, his fingers moving slowly, blood spreading beneath his body. Jake spared one brief thought about how he was going to clean it up. The deputy stared up at them, his mouth working as a small trickle of blood rolled down his grizzled chin.

"He's still breathing," Ruiz observed, his words more of a breathy gasp. Next to him Del stood, a silent warrior ready to act. Neither of them lowered their guns.

"That can change in an instant," Si said. At Mitch's silent gesture, he lowered his gun, along with everyone else, although he didn't look happy.

Mitch turned to Riley. "You gonna expect us to carry him to the hospital?"

"He can rot in hell." Riley snarled. All of the team nodded, including Jake.

They had dispensed fitting justice. The team stood over Marshall's body watching the deputy breathe his last. No one bent down to see if they could help the man who'd destroyed their team with one senseless act. If anyone held them to account—Jake mentally shrugged. If anyone objected they could go fuck themselves.

After shooting Marshall, Doug had rushed outside to find Carl. Howie sat with Moose, who was alive and grumbling that it was just a flesh wound.

Jake heard a cough behind them. Everyone turned except Si, who kept his eyes and weapon on Marshall. Doug, who'd done the coughing, approached the team. The bar regulars had hung back, seemingly understanding this was a moment the team needed by themselves. "The sheriff's here. Do we let him in?"

Fuck! They were going to have to explain it before Jake had got his head together.

"How are we going to explain we killed one of his team?" Del asked.

Mitch growled low in his throat. "At gun point if necessary. Jake, what do you want us to do?"

Jake looked back at Marshall's face. The man was taking his time to expire. "I'll talk to him outside first. Sheriff Clarkson's old school but I'm not sure how he's going to take this. Mitch, will you come with me?"

"Always," Mitch said instantly, and for a second they rubbed shoulders.

"And Doug?" Jake looked over his shoulder. "He'll take us more seriously if you're there. Sheriff Clarkson's trigger-happy, so no guns."

Mitch didn't look happy but Doug nodded, and the two men holstered their weapons, Doug carrying his shotgun. Jake stalked toward the door, Mitch and Doug on his heels.

Jake squinted, momentarily blinded by the afternoon sunshine as he stepped outside.

"Tyler, stay where you are. Hands up."

Sheriff Clarkson's bellowed order stopped Jake in his tracks. They were facing at least a dozen armed cops. "Sheriff." Jake raised his hands, keeping his movements calm.

"You armed?" Clarkson asked.

"Yes."

"Put your weapons on the ground—slowly."

Jake thought that was a bad move on the sheriff's part. He and Mitch could take out most of the cops in that one action, but he said, "Okay, don't shoot. Going to move my hands."

"Do it."

Jake, Mitch and Doug laid their guns on the floor and kicked them to one side, then raised their hands. The sheriff gestured and two other deputies, rushed forward, taking the weapons. They didn't seem anxious to cuff them yet.

"Carl and Moose are hurt, Sheriff. They need help now."

"We found Carl. He was awake and not happy. We sent him to the hospital. I thought the EMTs were gonna sedate him just to shut him up. I'll send people in to help Moose." He waved at EMTs who quickly rushed past them.

Jake breathed a sigh of relief that Carl was awake and grumbling. He'd be fine.

"Where's Marshall?" Sheriff Clarkson demanded.

Jake had no idea how the sheriff was going to take the news of his deputy's fate. "Dead. More or less," he said shortly.

The sheriff didn't seem surprised or angry at the news. Jake guessed Lukas had got there first. "You ain't sure, son? Thought you were meant to be the e-lite." He drawled out the first syllable.

Jake shifted his stance and noticed one of the deputies twitched. He stilled, catching the man's eye to show he meant no harm. "I shot him."

"And me," Mitch growled beside him.

"So did I." Doug added. "That bastard ain't never moving again. He's just taking his time meeting his maker."

Sheriff Clarkson's mouth worked a couple of times but he didn't say anything. Jake studied the other deputies. There were still a lot of frowns and weapons trained on them. He hoped none of them were best friends with Marshall. They stared back impassively, one or two of them chewing the cud.

Then Clarkson said, "And he's still not dead? You need more practice."

Jake felt Mitch's twitch of annoyance beside him, but they both kept quiet.

"He murdered your sister?" Clarkson asked finally.

Jake furrowed his brow, wondering where Clarkson had gotten that piece of information. He nodded at the sheriff. "Yes, sir."

"You're sure it was him?"

"He admitted it in front of all of us. You can take our statements."

Sheriff Clarkson grunted and looked at his men. At his nod they all lowered their weapons although they didn't relax. "We'll take statements later. And the escaped felon?"

"Riley?" Jake frowned.

"You got more than one in there, son?"

"He's here," Jake said curtly.

"My orders were to take him into custody and return him to jail."

Jake was about to protest even though he knew it was going to happen. Then he caught the sheriff's inflection.

"Were?"

"I got new orders. It's out of my hands. It's my understanding the felon needs medical attention. He's to be taken to the hospital first."

Mitch didn't look surprised and turned to Jake. "I'll call Lukas. Get the orders. If that's okay with the sheriff?" He waited for Clarkson to give his assent. There was a brief pause then the sheriff nodded.

"You can take your weapons, son."

Mitch grabbed his gun, as did Jake and Doug, then Mitch and Doug disappeared inside.

Jake holstered his gun and studied the sheriff warily. "You don't seem... bothered by Marshall's death."

Clarkson shrugged. "The man was a murderer and a thief. He has no business wearing the uniform. I got no truck with criminals in my force." He took off his hat, wiped the sweat from his brow and jammed it back on his head.

Jake nodded slowly. He'd always had a strained relationship with the sheriff, in no small part because he was a homo. But the sheriff appreciated how Jake treated his customers. Jake kept his nose clean and didn't break any of the rules.

"Let's see Marshall," Clarkson growled, stomping forward with two of his deputies falling in behind him. The rest of the police officers stayed where they were. Jake stood back and let the sheriff go in first.

One of the deputies, a handsome black guy a couple of inches shorter than Jake, stopped on the threshold and looked at him. "Sorry to hear about your sister, Mr. Tyler."

Jake blinked in surprise. "Uh... thanks, sir. Marshall...?"

The deputy hawked in his throat. "No loss."

He carried on through and Jake stared after him, shaking his head in surprise. Marshall didn't seem to have been popular in his new job. He obviously wouldn't be missed.

Inside, the EMTs were dealing with Moose, and Marshall's body was alone in the middle of the floor. Jake stayed by the door, waiting for Mitch to finish his call. A few minutes later, Mitch joined him.

"You all right, JT—Jake?"

Jake took his time to focus on Mitch, watching the man's strong throat work. "Yeah, I guess. No one seems that pissed about Marshall's death. Has he got a wife or a family?"

"I just called Lukas. He said Marshall had a fiancé. There was talk of domestic violence, but she'd never press any charges."

"The world's gonna be a better place without him," Jake said. He watched the EMTs shift Moose onto a stretcher. "Marshall's gone?"

The lead EMT nodded. "Yeah."

"'Bout time," Ruiz said. "Good riddance to bad fucking rubbish." And the rest of the team grunted in agreement.

Jake noticed Riley was nowhere in sight and nor was Si or the sheriff.

As they took Marshall's body, Jake breathed easier for the first time, as if something toxic in the air around him had been removed. He'd thought his life was settled when he bought the pub. Now Jake was facing the fact that *nothing* had been settled. That he'd just put Band-Aids over the gaping wounds in his head and heart. Now the Band-Aids had been ripped off and the pain oozed out.

Mitch squeezed his shoulder. "The sheriff wants our statements. He says it won't take long. Then you can open up again."

Jake took a deep breath and fleetingly leaned back against Mitch. "You guys gonna take down the plywood at the windows?"

Mitch grunted. “It’s safer with them on.”

“Take them down,” Jake muttered wearily.

“’Kay.” Mitch’s breath blew across Jake’s ear then he stepped away, leaving Jake feeling eerily alone.

“Mr. Tyler?” Jake looked over his shoulder. The deputy he’d spoken to at the door said, “Can we talk?”

Jake nodded and followed him to one of the booths in the far corner, walking around the large blood stain in the middle of the room. He slid into one side of the booth and the deputy sat on the other.

The deputy held out his hand and Jake shook it. The man had a firm handshake but he didn’t turn it into a pissing contest. “My name’s Deputy Charles Wright. I’m new to the sheriff’s office. I just need your statement.”

Jake inhaled sharply. “What do you need to know? Haven’t you got statements from the others?”

“They’re apparently off limits.” Wright didn’t sound impressed.

Jake gave a wry smile. “But not me?”

“Not you,” Wright agreed. “Let’s start at the beginning.”

“I need a drink if we’re going to do that.” Jake looked over at Howie who was behind the bar and talking to Si. “Howie, can we have two..., what do you want to drink?”

“Ice tea?”

“Two teas, Howie. Thanks.”

Howie saluted and headed into the kitchen, Si hot on his tail. Jake wondered if Si was going to be able to leave Howie behind when the team departed. The thought of them going depressed Jake more than he cared to admit.

Jake huffed and forced himself to pay attention to the deputy. “Can I ask you a question?”

Wright frowned. “What do you want to know?”

“Marshall’s not in uniform. How did he hear about Riley’s

escape?"

"Details were sent to us two days ago. Marshall was on duty when the information came in. Our clerk says Marshall called this morning to ask her to let him know if Riley was recaptured."

"You didn't think that was odd?"

"Not really. Riley was his collar. Nobody wondered why he wanted to get him back behind bars."

Jake nodded his head slowly. "So, when did you realize he was the bad guy?"

One side of Wright's mouth quirked up. "I'm supposed to be asking you the questions."

"Yeah." Jake reddened slightly. "I forgot about that."

Howie placed two glasses of tea in front of them, the condensation dripped down the glass. Wright took a long chug making a sound of satisfaction when he finally swallowed. "That's good."

Jake drank down half his glass and waited for Wright to start. Out of the corner of his eye he could see Mitch talking with the sheriff. He couldn't hear what they were saying but Mitch must have been aware of Jake's gaze upon him, because he turned and gave Jake a slight smile, the crinkles around his eyes and mouth deepening. Jake smiled back and then turned to the deputy as he started speaking.

"His former partner, Emilio Sanchez, confessed," Wright offered, despite the reminder that he was asking the questions.

"Confessed? Confessed to what?"

"He was caught stealing from a house this morning." Wright shrugged. "He confessed about the burglaries two years ago. Then he threw the murder into the mix. Sorry, your sister's murder."

"What the hell?" Jake couldn't remember much about

Marshall's former partner except that he was quiet compared to Marshall's loud brashness.

"I know. Raleigh PD called Sheriff Clarkson, but Marshall had already called about Riley. Sheriff put two and two together and came up with Marshall being a nasty piece of work. We knew Riley would be heading this way, so here we are."

Too late, Jake thought to himself but he just smiled through gritted teeth.

Wright cast him a shrewd look as if he had a clue what Jake was thinking. "Let's get down to business."

"Sure."

"Do you remember dialing 911 after finding your sister?"

Jake knuckled his eyes. "Yeah, I remember. Not a lot else afterward though," he added honestly. "Wait."

"Yes?"

Jake was aware of the impatience in Wright's voice but he had more questions. "How the hell did Marshall end up here? Was he stalking me?"

"He started the same time as I did. It's only supposition but I think he wanted to get away from Woodbridge. A fresh start. From the questions he asked dispatch, I don't think he had any idea you were here."

Jake shuddered at the thought that Marshall might have suddenly discovered he was living close by. He had a feeling his life expectancy would have shortened considerably.

"Can you remember how much time it took for the cops to arrive after you rang dispatch?"

"Five minutes. Maybe less."

"How do you know?" Wright demanded.

"I walked in just after 3.50. The cops were there by 4 p.m. I could see the kitchen clock ahead of me, and the game had just started."

Tick tock, tick tock.

"Did you think that was odd at the time?"

"No, sir." Jake thought back. He was trained to think, to observe, but all he could remember was the blood spilling from the knife that Riley held. "I'm sorry, I wasn't thinking about it at the time. I heard the sirens. The cops came in first and the EMTs a few minutes later. I was just glad they were there." The cops arrived, then the EMTs, then Mitch. Jake didn't even remember calling Mitch. He just remembered standing in the front yard, Mitch's arms around him. Wright coughed and Jake realized he'd been lost in his own thoughts. "Sorry, did you ask another question?"

Wright looked sympathetically at him. "It's been a long day, huh?"

"You have no idea," Jake murmured.

Finally, when the questions were finished, Jake escaped from the deputy's clutches. He found Mitch and Riley out back. Riley wasn't wearing cuffs now and they both looked up as he came out. Riley looked a little tentative, but Mitch just patted the seat next to him. Jake took a deep breath, straddled the seat and sat down. He raised one eyebrow at the large glasses of beer in front of them.

"I can't wait to see Lukas' face when you give him the bill for the food, drink and repairs," Mitch said, following Jake's gaze.

"You think he's gonna pay up?" Riley asked. He picked up his glass and took a long swallow. "God, that's good. My first beer in two years. Keep 'em coming."

"He'd better." Jake would personally ram the invoice down his former section leader's throat if Lukas caused a fuss. He looked at Riley. "What happens now?"

"We've just been talking about that," Mitch said. "He'll be taken into custody, then to the hospital first, then to the local jail. The sheriff is giving us a few minutes to talk."

"You were hit again?" Jake frowned as he studied Riley. He couldn't see any visible signs of injury apart from the bruise on his cheek. "You should've been checked over by the EMTs."

"I wasn't hit." Riley looked sour as he pressed his hands against his abdomen. "My fucking guts hurt, man."

Jake frowned. "Your guts? The appendicitis? It wasn't fake?"

"Not fake," Riley confirmed. "It's been rumbling for a few days and the prison doc wanted to get it looked at. When the accident happened, I didn't know what to do. But when I realized the guards were knocked out I had to escape."

"You escaped from the prison guards, traveled halfway across the country *and* got involved in a gun fight, with appendicitis?" Jake just stared at him. "Stop drinking that beer."

Riley reached for the glass but Jake snatched it from the table. "Hey, one beer ain't gonna kill me."

But Jake turned on Mitch. "Christ, Mitch, what were you thinking? Get him to the hospital right now. If that appendix bursts he's a goner. You're both fucking stupid in the head."

Mitch rolled his eyes. "Si's gone to get the SUV. Then we're going."

Jake got to his feet. "You're leaving now. I can take you."

"You're still a fucking mother-hen," Mitch grumbled, but he stood, too. "Come on, Riley. Jake can drive us."

Riley growled but he was a peculiar shade of green and, when he stood, he staggered slightly. Jake grabbed ahold of him in case he fell over. "How the hell did you get here?"

"Fucking luck, man. Fucking luck." Riley leaned against him.

Jake looked at Mitch. "We've got to go—*now*."

They each took one of Riley's arms and walked him around the building. As they reached the parking lot Si pulled up with the SUV. Mitch slid open the side door and jumped in then Jake helped Riley into the vehicle.

"You gonna hurl?" Jake asked as Riley settled on the back seat.

"Not sure," Riley admitted. "Can I think about it?"

"Wait a minute." Jake leapt out of the SUV, ignoring Mitch's grumbled, "I thought we had to go *now*?" He ran through the bar and into the kitchen, hunting for a large plastic mixing bowl. Then he made the return journey, waving off concerned questions from Howie and Doug. He jogged over to Del and Ruiz before he left the bar. "Riley's crashing. We're going to the hospital."

"Will he be okay?" Ruiz asked, concern written all over his face.

Jake shook his head. "No idea. I've got to go."

Del nodded. "Go. Go. We'll manage things here with Howie.

One nod and Jake ran to the SUV, holding out the bowl to Riley, who murmured his thanks and closed his eyes again.

"Aren't you coming?" Mitch asked as Jake made no move to get in the SUV.

"Do you want me to?"

Riley cracked open one eye and held out one shaking hand. "Please, Jake, I want you there."

Jake didn't hesitate. He climbed in, slid the door shut, and Si pulled away before Jake had sat down. Jake took Riley's hand in his. "I'm here, Riley. I'm here."

"Glad." Riley closed his eyes again and held on tight to Jake's hand as if it were a lifeline.

CHAPTER 11

On the twenty-mile journey to the hospital, Riley stayed quiet, groaning when the SUV hit a bump in the road. Jake held his hand all the way and Riley didn't let go. Mitch stayed silent for a long time and, eventually, Jake looked up to see the shell-shocked expression on his face.

Jake leaned over to touch Mitch's knee. "What's wrong. You look almost as white as Riley does."

"Riley was fine," Mitch muttered. "He was fine until you arrived. There was nothing wrong with him."

"I think he was running on pure adrenaline," Jake suggested. "Then I reminded him he was sick. Maybe his body took over, you know, gave him permission to be ill."

"I should've realized, but he didn't say anything."

"Wanted beer." Riley's mumble tailed off into a groan as they hit another bump.

"Christ, Si, are you gonna hit every bump in the highway?" Mitch snapped.

"Easy, easy," Jake said. "Riley can cope with a few bumps."

"Sorry," Si said, glancing briefly over his shoulder. "How is he?"

Riley managed to crack one eye open. "Feel like shit."

"Another ten minutes and we'll be there," Jake assured him.

"Good." The last vestiges of color drained from Riley's face and he clutched his belly.

Jake held Riley's hand tighter and gave Si directions to the hospital.

Ignoring all the parking restrictions, Si screeched up to the entrance of the ER. Mitch opened the door as the vehicle drew to a halt and jumped out. He helped Jake ease Riley out of the car and they half-carried him into the reception area. Mitch yelled for help.

A couple of nurses rushed toward them, assessing Riley's condition as he slumped in Jake and Mitch's arms, and led them to an empty cubicle. Riley collapsed on the bed and the nurse tried to shoo Mitch and Jake away, but neither of them were going anywhere and it soon became clear Riley wasn't up to answering questions.

The nurse started immediate observations. "What happened?"

"Appendicitis," Jake said.

The nurse raised her eyebrow. "You're a medic?"

"No," Jake said shortly. "A doctor was sending him to the hospital for tests a couple of days ago."

"Was sending? What happened?" she asked suspiciously. "Is this the escaped convict we got a notice about?"

For a while it looked like explanations about Riley's status as an escaped convict was going to take precedence over any treatment he received. Mitch looked like he was about to explode and Jake was about to threaten the nurse with bodily violence when Riley vomited over himself, the bed, the floor and the nurse's feet. As she was the one holding up his treatment, Jake and Mitch weren't sympathetic.

Tests confirmed Riley's appendix had ruptured and he needed immediate surgery. As they wheeled Riley away, Mitch called Lukas and got him to talk to the hospital. Their attitude changed abruptly, although Jake suspected it was more to do with the assurance the medical bills would be paid.

Jake stepped outside to call Sheriff Clarkson and look for Si, who hadn't followed them into the ER.

"Clarkson." The surprisingly light voice of the sheriff spoke after a couple of minutes.

"Sheriff? It's Jake Tyler."

"What can I do for you, Mr. Tyler?"

"We're at the hospital with Riley Ward. His appendix burst. Could you call and reassure them they don't have a murderer on their hands?"

"I'll do that now."

Jake took a deep breath and relaxed at the sheriff's assurance. "Thanks. Have you heard any more about Sanchez?" There was a pause and he could hear the sheriff talking to someone in the background. Then the sheriff spoke again.

"He's been booked for the burglaries and they're still talking to him about the murder."

"Will you keep me involved?"

"You mean your ex-team leader won't tell you first?"

Jake chuckled at the sheriff's dry retort although he didn't feel much like laughing. "Your guess is as good as mine."

"I'll call you as soon as I hear anything. How is Ward?"

"It's touch and go," Jake admitted. "The fact he even got here before the appendix ruptured is astounding."

"I'll pray for him," Clarkson said.

"Thank you, sir. I think he needs it."

Jake said goodbye to the sheriff. Si was still nowhere to be seen, so Jake walked back into the reception area. Mitch was slumped in a seat, his long legs stretched out in front of him and crossed at the ankles. His chin rested on his chest and his eyes were closed. Jake took the opportunity to study Mitch for a moment without being caught.

"What's happening?" Si said over Jake's shoulder.

"What happened to you?" Jake asked.

Si gave Jake a small shove toward the seats. "I went to park and call Howie. How's Riley?"

Jake growled at being shoved around but he moved in Mitch's general direction. "He's in surgery. His appendix ruptured."

"Fuck," Si cursed, then mouthed an apology at an elderly lady nearby. "Is he gonna make it?"

"How the fuck do I know?" It was Jake's turn to catch a scowl from the elderly lady. "Sorry, ma'am." The woman pursed her lips and huffed as she looked away.

Mitch opened his eyes at their approach. "Hey." He squinted at Si. "Where've you been? You only had to park the damn car."

Si rolled his eyes. "Jeez, I was gone for thirty minutes. I was talking to Howie. Have you heard from the docs?"

"He's fine, running around, and wants a steak dinner," Mitch said.

Jake blinked at Mitch. "Really?"

Now it was Mitch's turn to blink. "What the hell? You didn't really believe that?"

"He's not out of surgery yet?"

"Not unless they practice TV surgery here. Did you bash your head?"

Jake slumped down next to Mitch and kicked his ankle. "You're an asshole." He didn't bother to apologize to the woman again. She could move away if she was that offended.

Si looked around. "There's a vending machine over there. Do you want a coke?" He patted his pockets. "Damn, I didn't bring my wallet."

"Sure." Jake dug in his pockets and brought out a handful of change. "Use this."

"Great." Si scooped the money out of Jake's hand.

He walked off without asking them what they wanted. But when he came back with two cans of Pepsi and one Dr. Pepper, their usual drinks of choice, Jake guessed Si didn't need to. He took one of the Pepsis and popped the top. Mitch chugged back most of the Dr. Pepper in a few swallows and exhaled in satisfaction.

They sat for what felt like the entire night but was probably only two hours. Mitch was warm and close-by, and although they weren't touching, his proximity was enough to calm Jake's nerves. At one point he must have fallen asleep because he woke up when Mitch moved and discovered that not touching was moot. He'd been sleeping on Mitch's shoulder.

Jake sat up and knuckled his eyes. "Huh? S'done yet?" He looked around to see a new group of people had joined them since he fell asleep.

Mitch quirked one side of his mouth. "You finally woke up."

"Yeah, sorry. How long was I asleep?" Jake looked around. "Where's Si?"

"He was fretting about Howie, Riley and driving me nuts so I sent him back to JT's. I promised to call him if we heard anything." Mitch's voice was rough and frustrated. He smiled at Jake. "At least you were asleep and quiet."

Jake waited.

"Apart from the snoring."

If Jake hadn't been in public, he would've poked his tongue out. "Thanks."

"And the drooling."

Jake decided the public could go hang.

"You're welcome." Mitch tipped an imaginary hat.

Jake chuckled and Mitch joined in, then their laughter

died away. Jake's mouth dried up. Fuck, they were in public. In public, waiting for news on Riley and Jake would've happily jumped Mitch right this second. From the look on Mitch's face he felt the same way.

"Is anyone here for Riley Ward?"

Saved by the fucking bell. Jake could've kissed the elderly scrubs-clad nurse calling out for them.

"Here," Mitch said gruffly.

They got to their feet and approached the nurse. She blinked at them, taking in their size. "Is one of you JT?"

Jake nodded. "That's me, ma'am. Jake Tyler."

"You're his family?"

"I'm his brother-in-law."

"And I'm his boss," Mitch said, his tone making it clear he wasn't going to be left behind.

She furrowed her brow and Jake was relieved when she didn't feel the need to ask more questions. "He's out of surgery. It was touch and go for a while, but he's going to be all right."

"Can we see him?" Mitch asked.

"Just for five minutes. He really needs to get some rest."

They followed her down a hallway, walking shoulder to shoulder. Just for an instant Mitch's hand brushed Jake's and they entangled little fingers. The touch comforted Jake. He was going to miss this when Mitch returned home. As the nurse paused outside a door, Mitch let go of Jake's hand.

"You can go in one at a time. Five minutes only."

Mitch gently pushed Jake toward the door. "You go first."

Jake followed the nurse into the room. Riley was hooked up to several machines, all of them looked scary.

"Hey." He touched Riley's hand.

Riley opened his eyes, taking a moment to focus. He looked puzzled as he mumbled, "Hey."

"How do you feel?"

"Stoned," Riley said, and gave Jake a lopsided grin. "Best I've felt in forever." Then the grin slid off his face. "What happened?"

"Remember your appendix?."

"Oh." Riley nodded absently. "Is this the prison infirmary?"

Jesus, he really was stoned. "Riley, what do you remember?"

"My guts hurt." Riley raised his head to look down. "They don't hurt now. JT, why are you here? You hate me."

Jake sighed and held Riley's hand. "I don't hate you, Riley. Go back to sleep."

"Didn't kill Sharon." Riley's voice trailed off and Jake thought he was asleep until he said, "Love her."

"I know you do, buddy. I know you do."

Jake watched Riley sleep for a few minutes then he rejoined Mitch in the hallway.

"How is he?" Mitch asked.

"Out of it," Jake said. "He's sleeping now. He doesn't remember the last couple of days. He thinks he's still in prison."

Mitch looked pained. "Poor guy."

"What's going to happen to him now? Is he going back to prison?" Jake couldn't face the thought of Riley being sent back to jail.

Mitch shrugged. "It's in Lukas' hands, not mine. He's got to face the consequences of escaping."

"He's been locked up for a crime he didn't commit and now he's in a hospital bed."

"I know. But you know Lukas is the best person to sort it out. He's not going to let Riley out of the team's sight if he can help it."

To his horror, Jake felt tears well up and he turned away, on the pretense of looking at Riley. He didn't want Mitch to see how upset he was. It wasn't just about Riley, or the attack on the bar, or the realization that Sharon's killer had finally faced justice. It was about having to face up to his feelings for the man he'd run away from.

Then Mitch laid a hand on his shoulder and turned Jake in his arms. "Come here."

Jake shuddered once, then he buried his face in Mitch's shirt and let the tears flow. Mitch enfolded Jake in his embrace and they stayed like that for long moments while the emotions of the last few years got the better of him.

"What happened? Is he dead? Jeez, you said he was all right!" Si's horrified voice made Jake raise his head.

"What the hell?" Mitch muttered, sounding annoyed as Jake took a step back and wiped his eyes.

Si looked as if he was on the edge of tears himself. "You said he was all right!"

"He is all right, douchebag." Mitch pointed to Riley. "Look, you can see for yourself. He's asleep."

Si turned to check then he looked at Jake. "Why are you crying then? Is this some gay shit? Am I going to start crying now?"

"Shut the fuck up," Jake muttered. It was bad enough he had cried in public without Si bellowing it to the whole world.

Mitch drew Jake against his side. "Just ignore him."

"*Me*? Ignore *me*?" Si huffed and acted like he was outraged, but then he tugged Jake away from Mitch and against his solid body. Jake stumbled and it was only Si's solid stance that kept them both on their feet.

"Fuck, Si," Jake grumbled, but he allowed Si to hug him for a moment before he pulled away.

Si grinned and tweaked Jake's nose. "Too late. Howie's

claimed me. And Mitch would have my balls if I touched you."

"You've just put your hands all over me." Jake stepped back out of Si's reach, using Mitch as a shield.

"You loved it. So, when can I see Riley?"

Mitch sighed. "I suddenly realize how quiet it's been the last two years. There's no nurse in sight. Go in for five minutes. Don't wake him up." His tone suggested he didn't believe Si would take the slightest notice. Si went into Riley's room, sat down beside him, and took Riley's hand. "He's missed him."

"They were partners," Jake said, watching Riley and Si. "I'm surprised Del and Ruiz aren't here."

Mitch checked his phone. "They're on their way. I thought they'd be here by now."

Five minutes later, the reason for their delay became clear. Behind the dark heads of Del and Ruiz was a blond-haired man, tall and slender, his stride purposeful. When Lukas reached them, for the third time in ten minutes, Jake found himself being hugged and close to tears once more.

Lukas held him tight, muttering into his ear. "Don't you dare run away again, Jake Tyler—ever."

Jake held onto him, shaken by his calm and controlled section leader's show of emotion. "I won't. It's good to see you, Lukas."

Finally, Lukas collected himself enough to step away. "What's the sitrep with Riley?"

Distracted by Lukas, Jake hadn't realized Ruiz and Del had slipped into Riley's room, ignoring all the rules. Jake looked at Mitch and Lukas, and nodded to the door.

"Oh, hell yes," Mitch said.

Lukas didn't respond. He was already going through the door to join the others. Jake and Mitch followed him.

Riley opened his eyes and blinked in confusion at the crowd around his bed. His gaze flitted from one man to the next, barely focusing until he spotted Lukas. "Sir? Why are you here?" Then Riley furrowed his brow. He tried to speak, coughed, and tried again. "Guys? Where am I?"

Taking charge—as usual—Lukas stepped up to the head of the bed and took Riley's' hand. "You're in the hospital, Ward."

"Am I going back to prison?" Riley asked.

"Do you remember anything about the last two days?"

Riley frowned then he shook his head. "I had a bellyache and the prison doc said I had to go to the hospital. That's all I remember." He looked at Jake. "I didn't kill Sharon. You've got to understand. I didn't do it."

Lukas squeezed his hand. "It's okay. We know."

"You do?" Riley asked doubtfully. His gaze snapped back to Jake. "You believe me?"

Jake joined Lukas so that Riley could focus on him. "We know it was Marshall."

"Marshall?"

"The police officer who was first on the scene. He and his partner were responsible for a string of burglaries in the area. They targeted your house and Sharon was just in the wrong place at the wrong time. I'm so sorry, Riley."

Riley raised a shaking hand and wiped his eyes. "I didn't think you'd ever believe me."

Jake was gutted. He wanted to apologize but as he opened his mouth to speak he was interrupted by an outraged voice.

"What on earth? I said one person for five minutes. Not a family gathering."

The team turned as one to face the door. Jake was on the point of telling the nurse to take a long walk off a short pier, and he had a feeling he wasn't the only one. Fortunately,

Lukas intervened before one of them said something stupid and got them all thrown out.

"I'm sorry. It's the first time we've all been together for a long time. Riley is very important to us." Lukas smiled at the nurse and her angry expression faded a little.

"I understand, but he's just had a major operation. Mr. Ward needs time to recover."

Riley yawned as if he agreed.

"We'll go. He needs to sleep." Lukas held his hand up at the protests from the team. "We'll stay two at a time. Jake, do you want to stay first?"

Mitch said, "I'm staying with him," before Jake could answer.

"That's fine. We'll go back to the bar." Lukas said.

Jake decided not to argue. He wanted to spend as much time by Mitch's side as possible before the team left. One by one, the team took their leave, shaking Riley's hand.and promising they'd be back later.

Si was the last, but he took both of Riley's hands in his, saying, "I'll be back later, partner."

"I'm still your partner?" Riley blinked at him sleepily. "You haven't got a new partner?"

"No one matched up to you." Si gave Riley a wobbly smile and left the room. Jake had a feeling Si needed a dark corner to get himself together.

Jake looked at the nurse, who was still standing by the door. "I'm his brother-in-law. I want to stay with him."

She held the door open. "Stand outside for a few minutes then you can come back in."

Jake was about to argue because he'd just got through telling the nurse he wasn't going anywhere, but Mitch shoved Jake toward the door.

"What the—?"

Jake tried to dig in, but Mitch just looked over his shoulder. “We’ll be back soon, Riley.”

“’Kay. Don’t be long.” Riley gave another wide yawn and closed his eyes.

The door closed behind them and Jake turned on Mitch. “What the hell?”

Mitch drew him to one side of the hall, out of sight of the room. “We make nice with the nurse so she lets us stay here. If we make a fuss, she’ll throw us out and Riley will be alone. Just take a deep breath and do what the nurses want. Okay?” He held Jake’s gaze until finally Jake nodded. “Okay then. Let’s get coffee.”

“Hospital coffee is disgusting.”

Jake grumbled all the way along the hall until Mitch threatened to pick Jake up and shove him in the nearest trash receptacle if he didn’t stop complaining.

CHAPTER 12

Four hours later Si and Lukas replaced them. Mitch took a deep breath as they walked out of the hospital. "Let's go eat."

"We have food back at the bar," Jake pointed out. He waited at Mitch's side.

"I need some time alone with you." Mitch's roughly growled confession left stirrings in Jake's groin.

Jake needed time with Mitch, too. "Where can we go?"

"Steak with all the fixin's?" Mitch sounded as if his mouth was watering.

"At this time of night?"

Mitch nodded. "I talked to one of the nurses. There's a steakhouse nearby that stays open because of the hospital."

"Lead on."

The maître d' took one look at Jake and Mitch, and led them to a booth at the back of the restaurant. Normally Jake would've been annoyed at being clocked so easily, but he was too tired to care. They slid into the booth and Jake took a deep breath as he leaned back against the corner. He closed his eyes for a moment while Mitch ordered for them both immediately when the waitress arrived. Jake was so hungry he could've eaten the entire cow if it had been on the table.

Once the waitress walked away, Jake opened his eyes. Mitch was staring at him, his midnight blue gaze intense. Mitch flushed when he realized he'd been caught. "I can't quite believe you're here," Jake murmured.

Mitch answered, his voice just as low. "I don't want to take my eyes off you in case you vanish again."

That hurt Jake like a stab to the heart. He wondered if it would ever stop hurting. "I'm sorry, Mitch. I wish I could make it better."

"I'm sorry, too," Mitch said. "I shouldn't have let you go. I should've forced Lukas to give me your address."

"I asked him not to."

Mitch pressed his lips together so thinly Jake could barely see his mouth. "He would have if I'd forced the issue."

"No, he wouldn't."

"He would," Mitch's fingers twitched as if he had a weapon in his hand.

Jake shook his head. "You know Lukas. He'd shoot you rather give away team secrets." He sat up and tangled his legs with Mitch's. "Lukas knew I couldn't deal with you."

"But why?" Mitch asked. "I keep asking but I still don't understand. Why couldn't you talk to me?"

"I don't know that I can explain."

"Try," Mitch said, his tone and stare flat.

Jake laid his hands on the table. "I needed a partner. You were my team leader but not my partner."

"That's not true." Mitch sounded betrayed but he'd asked and now Jake had told him the truth.

"Yes, it is. We weren't out to the team. That was your decision and I respected it. But once Sharon died you were so busy keeping the team together, you didn't notice I was falling apart." Jake had been dying from the inside out and Mitch hadn't seen it.

"So, you're saying it's my fault?" Mitch demanded. "You walked because I wasn't paying enough attention to you?"

"I didn't say that."

"What *are* you saying then?"

Jake huffed impatiently. “It wasn’t about you. It was about me. I needed something and you couldn’t—or wouldn’t—give it to me.”

Mitch ran his hands through his hair, leaving it sticking up every which way. “But you didn’t *tell* me what you needed.”

“I don’t think I could’ve told anyone what I needed, not then.”

“Not even Lukas?”

“Not even him.”

They stared at each other, then the waitress appeared with their steaks. Mitch growled in frustration, but that turned into a groan when he took the first mouthful.

“This. Is. So. Good.”

Mitch moaned again and Jake gave him a raised eyebrow. “Are you eating or coming?”

“I’m not sure. This is orgasmic.” Mitch virtually inhaled the steak. He hadn’t touched the baked potato.

“Do you want another steak?”

“M’okay.” Mitch just kept eating… and eating.

Jake had forgotten how much Mitch ate after an assignment. He would barely eat until the action was over, but the second the mission was finished he would eat enough for three men. He waved at the waitress who came over.

“Another steak for my friend please.”

She watched Mitch demolish the food in front of him. “Just the one? I’m on it.” She and Jake shared a conspiratorial grin and she disappeared in the direction of the kitchen.

“She’s gonna think I’m a pig.” Mitch spoke before he took another mouthful of food.

Jake shrugged. “Who cares? You need the food, she gets a good tip, and Lukas pays. Win-win all round.”

People from nearby tables looked over as Mitch burst out laughing. "I missed you. Not just because of… us, but being on the team. You used to make Lukas rage, and the rest of us laugh."

Jake's lips twitched. "Do you remember when I planted grass seed on his carpet and then watered it?"

Mitch wiped the tears from his eyes. "I thought he was going to kill you when you offered to mow his office."

"He nearly fired me." Jake grimaced as he remembered Lukas' epic meltdown as he surveyed the neat lawn that had grown in the office while he was away. "I had to pay for a replacement carpet."

"The office would've contributed if you'd asked. It would've been worth it just for the look on his face." Mitch grinned at him for a moment then the smile slipped. "Once you left we stopped laughing."

"I think we all stopped laughing," Jake said quietly.

"Especially Riley."

Jake rubbed his jaw. "What're we gonna do with him, Mitch?"

"He's not going back to jail."

"Agreed." Jake would handcuff himself to Riley rather than let him spend one more night in a cell.

"We really need to talk to Lukas."

"I destroyed his life." Jake would never forgive himself for getting an innocent man, his best friend, his family, jailed.

"No." Mitch glared at him, his eyes snapping with anger. "You've got to stop talking like that. It's not your fault, Jake."

Jake appreciated the effort but he had to face up to what he'd done. He'd never be able to look at himself in the mirror otherwise. "How can you say that? It was my testimony that got him arrested."

"You saw him holding the knife over Sharon's body. We'd

have all made that error."

"Most of you didn't believe he was guilty."

"But we didn't prove he wasn't. If he's going to be angry it should be at me and Lukas for not defending him." Mitch pushed the remains of the food around his plate as if he'd lost his appetite. "We all fucked up, Jake. Not just you."

The waitress approached the table, her professional smile dimming when she saw the expression on the two men's faces. "Your steak? Is everything okay with the food?"

Jake took a deep breath and smiled at her. "Everything's fine."

She placed the steak in front of Mitch and escaped as quickly as she could, casting a doubtful look over her shoulder as she went.

Mitch stared at the red meat. "I don't think I'm that hungry now."

"Eat!" Jake said firmly, pushing the plate toward Mitch. "You need the food."

Mitch stabbed the meat with his fork and put it on his plate. "I miss the way you used to look after me."

"I miss looking after you. Even when you said I was fussing over you I knew you liked it." Jake watched Mitch slice a piece of meat and pop it into his mouth. The way Mitch slowly chewed had Jake shifting uncomfortably in his seat. Christ, he found Mitch eating sexy? That was so sad.

Mitch raised an eyebrow. "Have I got steak between my teeth?"

Jake flushed and looked down at his plate. He should've ordered steak for himself. He obviously had a thing for red meat.

Back at the bar, they discovered Lukas, Del and Ruiz had left for the hospital to replace Si and Howie and the bar was empty apart from them. Despite the fact that the danger was over, Jake didn't bother heading for his bed. He and Mitch rolled into their sleeping bags. Mitch pulled Jake into his arms and held him tight against him. Jake leaned back into his warmth.

"I still love you." Mitch's words breathed into Jake's ear.

Jake tilted his head to breathe into Mitch's mouth. "I love you, too." He rolled over to kiss Mitch more firmly, his hands grasping Mitch's biceps. "I never stopped loving you."

Mitch tugged him closer, one hand on Jake's ass, and one tangled through Jake's hair. "I never thought I'd see you again." He peppered Jake's face with hot kisses. "Every day I woke up and for a split second everything was all right. Then I'd see the empty pillow and I'd remember you weren't there."

Jake buried his hot face in Mitch's neck. "It was the same for me," he confessed, his lips moving against Mitch's rough, warm skin. "There was never anyone else. Only you." Mitch's hands tightened painfully on his skin, but Jake welcomed the pain, needed it to ground him.

They kissed for what felt like hours, mouths meeting, lips parting and tongues exploring, until they had to pull apart to breathe. Even then they didn't pull away from each other, staying as close as they could just to get oxygen. Jake wanted to push into Mitch's skin, to be absorbed by him, and never to come out again.

"I'm never going to let you go," Mitch growled against his mouth.

Jake didn't say anything. Couldn't. He felt the same way but he knew it was impossible. Their lives were separate now.

Mitch growled again at Jake's lack of response and he pushed Jake onto his back, stretching out over him and resting on his elbows by Jake's head. Jake's legs were still tangled in the sleeping bags but he didn't care, welcoming the feel of Mitch's body pressing into him. Mitch kept kissing him, until Jake's cheeks and chin were raw with the rasp of Mitch's stubble, his mouth puffy and tender.

One more kiss, then another until Jake squirmed underneath Mitch. He needed more than kisses. He wanted... no... demanded, Mitch inside him, fucking him. Jake slid his hands to the front of Mitch's waistband, fumbling with the button and zipper. Finally, he managed to get them undone, slip into Mitch's boxer briefs and press the palm of his hand against the hard, hot length of Mitch's cock. Mitch shoved his hips against Jake's hand, demanding and needy, wanting more than a light squeeze. Jake was happy to oblige, cupping Mitch's velvety balls for a moment before sliding his hand up to enfold Mitch's shaft.

"Fuck." Mitch let out a breathy curse as Jake tugged his cock.

"Want you, too," Jake agreed on a rising gasp.

Mitch sat up and distentangled himself from his sleeping bag then he dragged Jake's sleeping bag off and threw it to one side. They both shoved their tac pants and briefs down their legs and then rolled back, rubbing their groins together. Jake gasped again at the feel of Mitch pressed against him. Their thighs tangled, rough hair against rough hair. Jake's senses were on fire. He had Mitch's hoarse breath in his ear, his rough hands on Jake's arms and his hips pressing into Jake's. There was nothing soft or gentle about this coupling. Jake needed Mitch and Mitch sure as hell needed Jake from the way he was hanging onto him.

Jake groaned as Mitch leaned over them, nudging Jake's fingers aside and wrapping his larger hand around both their cocks. "Fuck, that feels good."

Mitch slowly jacked them until Jake was squirming

against him. Velvet hard friction against velvet hard friction. Mitch swiped his thumb across the head of Jake's cock, spreading the pre-come over them both.

Jake groaned loudly. "You've gotta stop. I'm gonna come."

Mitch's lips twitched and Jake knew if he could see him, he'd see the amusement in his eyes. "That's the point."

Jake shook his head. "I wanna come with you inside me."

Mitch sucked in a breath. "Fuck."

"Now," Jake agreed.

"Lube and rubbers?"

"My wallet." Jake flung out a hand, looking for his pants.

Mitch reached over and grabbed the pants. His movement made them both hiss as they rubbed together. He fumbled in the pockets and pulled out Jake's battered, black leather wallet. Mitch hesitated for a moment and Jake realized what the problem was.

"You bought it for me," he said quietly, closing his hands over Mitch's. "I couldn't throw it away."

"Thanks." Mitch's voice was low and hoarse. "Here."

Jake took the wallet from Mitch and fished out the small condom and lube packets. He hoped they were still in date. He'd put them in his wallet in a rare fit of optimism months ago, and there they'd stayed—unused and untouched. Jake handed them to Mitch. "Please?"

Mitch nodded and bent to kiss Jake, gently this time. "Are they still in date?"

Jake growled against his lips. "Were you reading my mind?"

"Maybe." Mitch chuckled a little.

Jake heard a crinkling sound then something cold pressed against his hole. "You could've warmed–ah!" He closed his eyes and took a deep breath as Mitch pressed one finger in. It had been a long while since Jake had been fucked. Since Mitch. And this was gonna burn.

"I'll go slowly," Mitch promised.

He moved his finger until Jake was breathing again. Then added another. Jake arched up and pressed against Mitch's palm. "Feels so good. Feels so good."

Mitch hummed in agreement. "You look good, baby." He pumped his fingers in and out until Jake writhed languorously, begging Mitch for more. Finally, Mitch rolled the condom down his dick and slathered on more lube. He arranged Jake's legs over his shoulders and Jake groaned as Mitch touched the head of his cock to Jake's hole.

When Mitch hesitated, Jake frowned up at him. "What's wrong?"

Mitch stroked the inside of Jake's thighs. "There's nothing wrong. You are never wrong. I just need to take my time." Mitch eased in an inch at a time until he was pressed flush against Jake's body.

Jake closed his eyes, needing to wallow in the feel of Mitch's body in his, trapping Jake's swollen shaft between them. He could feel the stickiness on his skin as his cock leaked in anticipation. Mitch moved, pulling back then pushing in. Jake gasped and pulled Mitch down for a dirty kiss, hard mouths mauling each other. Mitch moved again, sending sparks across Jake's prostate. They gasped into each other's mouths.

"Fuck me," Jake demanded.

Mitch sat up, hauled Jake's ass against him and thrust in harder. Sweat prickled across Jake's temples. He hung on and let Mitch fuck him. Jake's orgasm settled in his lower back, coiling there, ready to explode. He dug into Mitch's biceps, knowing he would leave bruises and reveling in the knowledge. One more glide over his sweet spot and that called it. Jake yelled as he came, spurting against his belly and chest. Mitch pulled out suddenly, making Jake cry out. He ripped off the condom, jacked himself and climaxed over Jake, their fluid mixing on Jake's heated flesh. Mitch collapsed onto the floor beside Jake, his chest heaving up and down as he gasped for air.

Jake felt empty and wanted Mitch back inside him. He tangled his fingers in Mitch's. "I love you."

"Always," Mitch replied, holding tightly to Jake's hand.

CHAPTER 13

Jake awoke to the sound of a ringing phone. He sat up, blinking sleepily, not entirely sure where the sound was coming from. He nudged Mitch, who growled and rolled over onto his stomach. Jake took a moment to admire Mitch's ass then nudged him again. "Mitch? Is that your phone?"

Mitch cracked open one eye. "Huh?"

"Your phone? It's ringing."

Jake watched in amusement as Mitch waved an arm somewhere in the direction of his pants. Jake leaned over him and pulled Mitch's phone out of his pocket. From the snoring snort that left Mitch's lips, there was no point in giving him the phone. He pressed connect. "Yeah?"

"Jake?" Lukas sounded startled.

"Yeah. Mitch is asleep. What can I do for you?"

"Riley's awake and asking for you."

"We're on our way. How is he? Where's Si and Howie?" Jake shoved Mitch. "Wake up!"

Mitch grunted and stayed asleep, his face and body relaxed.

"Riley's being a pain in the ass. Si and Howie went back to Howie's place to sleep," Lukas said. "They're on their way back here."

"Okay, we're on our way. Once I've thrown cold water over my glorious team leader."

"My?" Lukas asked.

Mitch opened his eyes, his midnight blue gaze fixed on Jake. "My?"

Jake flipped him off. "Slip of the tongue. Get up before I throw water over you."

Still grumbling, Mitch finally shifted his ass and got to his feet.

"He's standing even if his eyes aren't open. I can drive. We'll be there soon," Jake said. As Lukas said goodbye and disconnected the call, Jake got to his feet. He looked down at himself and grimaced. "Shit, I'm a mess. I've got to change before we go."

Mitch wrinkled his nose. "Go have a shower. You stink of come."

"Thanks." Jake picked at flakes on his clothes and sniffed. "Yeah, you're right. You can make coffee."

They stood, looking at each other. They were both naked from the waist down. Jake watched as Mitch's cock stiffened. His was doing the same.

Eventually, after the long pause stretched on and on, Mitch growled low in his throat. "Fuck! Go and shower now, or I'm going to bend you over the bar and fuck you senseless."

"Or I'll fuck you." It was meant to be a joke, but Mitch's gaze grew heated. There had never been an issue about who fucked who. It had been easy, a mutual feeling, whoever had needed it—fuck or be fucked.

"Go!"

Jake fled, knowing Mitch didn't make idle threats. He headed for the shower, stripped off his clothes and dumped them in the bathroom hamper. The hot water was welcome and refreshing. He stood under the stream letting the water run down his face and body. Jake could have stayed in the shower for hours, but he knew they had to get moving. He grabbed the shower gel and squeezed some into his palm, inhaling the citrus smell to help him wake up.

"Coffee," Mitch said.

Jake stuck one hand out of the shower. Mitch didn't make a comment about drinking it in the shower, he just handed Jake the mug. Jake slurped and sighed happily.

"Feeling better?" Outside the shower curtain, Mitch sounded amused.

"Ask me when you give me the second mug."

"You get that when we're on the road." Mitch ignored Jake's groan. "Hurry up."

He left the bathroom and Jake leant against the tiled wall, finishing off the coffee as quickly as he could.

Despite his words, Mitch took ten minutes to have a shower. While he got dressed Jake made more coffee and filled his large silver thermos flask.

"Ready?"

Jake looked over his shoulder to see Mitch standing in the doorway. His cock twitched as they locked eyes. He had always been as horny as hell when he laid eyes on Mitch post-shower. He was barefoot and wearing jeans, resting low-down on his hips, rather than his tac pants. Mitch's hair was wet, slick and droplets of water caught in his chest hair. Jake wanted to reach over and capture each drop with his tongue.

"Almost," Jake said. "Five minutes?"

Mitch nodded and headed back to the bar to finish getting dressed.

Jake took a deep breath. He tried to pour more coffee but his hands trembled and drops spilled down the side of the thermos. The bastard had done that deliberately, knowing how he would react. Jake pressed his palm against his cock. He was as hard as fuck and needed release but he took another breath. He'd have to wait for a minute before he could walk.

Jake handed Mitch coffee as Mitch drove to the hospital. Mitch took a long gulp then gave Jake a quick glance.

"We used to do this all the time."

"Drink coffee or drive?"

"Both."

Jake looked away. Mitch didn't say another word and the rest of the journey was taken in silence. After a couple of miles, Mitch entangled his fingers in Jake's. Jake left them there, needing the warm connection.

The police officer outside Riley's room stood back to let Jake and Mitch in when they arrived. The number of big men around Riley's bed blocked the patient from their view. When Jake and Mitch walked in Riley was protesting loudly about something.

"You've got no choice, Lukas. Just let them take me back."

"No fucking way." Si stabbed a finger at Riley. "Shut the fuck up."

"You can't let them do that, Lukas." That was Del. He sounded as angry as Si, just at a lower decibel level.

"I'm working on it." Lukas sounded calm, but Si starting shouting again.

"Not good enough. Not fucking good enough."

"Si, shh." Howie took Si into his arms. Si would have shrugged anyone else violently out of his hold, but he wouldn't do that to Howie.

"But—"

"Get yourself under control." Lukas pressed his lips together. He looked at Jake and Mitch. "Where the hell have you been?"

"Don't start," Mitch said wearily.

Jake ignored everyone to look at Riley. The man looked as if he'd been dragged through a ditch; his face was pale, his eyes glazed. The bruise on his cheek stood out in stark relief. His ankles and one wrist were cuffed to the bed. "You look like shit."

Riley's lips quirked up at one side. "Thanks."

"You're welcome." Jake glanced at Lukas. "So, what's all the shouting about?"

"The sheriff came by this morning to tell us the prison is on the way to collect Riley. He's going back to jail for escaping. They'll be here tomorrow."

Jake turned on Lukas. "You can't let this happen."

Lukas narrowed his eyes and pointed at Jake. "Don't you start."

But Riley said, "Everyone needs to calm the fuck down. I *did* escape from custody and I'm gonna hafta answer for that. It's okay. I can deal with that. What's another couple of months?"

"It's not fucking right," Ruiz muttered and there was a wave of agreement.

Jake was so tense his jaw ached with the strain of not bitching at Lukas, but it must have been obvious to at least one person in the room because Mitch rubbed low circles on his lower back.

Lukas still looked pissed off at the waves of resentment being aimed in his direction. "I'm already talking to a judge and the district attorney's office. Riley, you're gonna have to go back to jail, but I will get you freed soon."

"He's not going anywhere without us," Si insisted.

"You're going back to work or you're fired," Lukas snapped. "Riley isn't going anywhere today. He's not well enough to be discharged yet."

Si looked as if he was about to tell his section leader what to do with his order, but Mitch wisely intervened.

"We'll stay with Riley as long as we can; until there's a

new assignment."

Lukas pressed his lips together but he gave a sharp nod. "Fine. As long as Riley agrees."

Jake turned to look at Riley and burst out laughing. The others starting chuckling, too. Riley was fast asleep with his mouth open and, as they watched, he emitted a light snore. The sound of their amusement didn't wake him up.

Si took a photo. No one stopped him because blackmail material was always useful. Then Lukas shooed them out of the room.

Back in the hallway, Mitch drew Jake against him. Del yawned and Ruiz squeezed his shoulder.

Jake yawned in sympathy and, when his jaw unlocked, he said, "Why don't you go back to the bar? Mitch and I can stay with him."

"You should go. I'm staying with Riley." Lukas tapped on his phone. "I've got phone calls to make."

Si shook his head vigorously and although Howie looked dubious he also nodded. "I'm not going anywhere."

"Neither are we," Ruiz said.

Lukas huffed impatiently. "You're gonna be a pain in my ass."

"When have they ever been any different?" Mitch flipped off the outraged comments aimed at him. "We're going for breakfast. Jake, Del and Ruiz, come with me now. Si and Howie, you stay with Riley. If the Feds arrive, you call."

Lukas raised his eyebrow. "Do you have plans for *me*?"

Mitch crooked his fingers at Lukas. "You're coming with us."

"Who's the boss here?" Lukas asked. "Wait, don't answer that."

Si and Howie settled beside the sleeping man. Si had a set look on his face which didn't bode well for any officer who might try to take Riley away.

Jake smiled at Mitch. “You go on. I just want to talk to Howie.” At Si’s sharp look, Jake said, “Down boy, I just want to talk to my co-owner.” Both Si and Mitch didn’t look happy but Jake ignored them. Howie got up and followed Jake into the corridor away from the police officer still hovering outside the door. Jake waited until the other guys left then he looked up at Howie. “We haven’t had a chance to talk.”

Howie scuffed at the floor. “You’re worrying.”

“Yeah.” Jake leaned back against the wall and folded his arms. “I just don’t want you to launch into something you’re not ready for.”

“You don’t have to worry.” Howie poked Jake’s shoulder. “You’re like an old mother-hen.”

“Don’t you start.”

Howie sighed and squeezed Jake’s bicep. “I know this is fast, and I’m bemused by it, too. But Si’s going home soon and then who knows what’ll happen?”

“You seem very laid-back about it,” Jake said.

“Not really.” Howie gave him a sweet smile. “But Si is a good man. He’ll take care of me. Now, can we stop having this conversation? I’m not your son.”

Jake rolled his eyes. “I’m never going to stop worrying about you, or Mitch, or Riley, or any of the team.”

Howie dragged Jake into a bear hug. “At some point you’ll have to let us grow up.”

“Never going to happen. Jesus Christ, let me go, you great big ape.” Jake thumped on Howie’s back to get him to let go.

Howie squeezed harder then released him. “I’ll get back to Si and Riley. Go have breakfast.”

Jake held him for a moment before he nodded. “You’re a good man, Howie.”

“I know.” Howie smiled again and disappeared into the

hospital room.

The team looked up as Jake approached them. It was kind of creepy the way they all turned as one. Like dogs expecting a treat. Jake was tempted to ask them for a paw.

Lukas fixed him with a piercing look. “How’s Riley?”

Jake squeezed in next to Mitch. “He’s still asleep.”

“Everything okay between you and Howie?” Mitch asked, his voice a rumble in Jake’s ear. They were pressed close, their thighs against each other, generating warmth.

“Yeah. Although I still think this thing between him and Si is bizarre.”

Jake wasn’t the only one from the nods around the table, but Del just shrugged. “Si is a man of many layers.”

Ruiz furrowed his brow. “Many layers? You mean like peeling an onion?”

Mitch snorted. “If you start talking like Donkey, that’s it. I’ve had it.”

Del threw a piece of biscuit across the table at Mitch. “I’m not a fucking donkey.”

Mitch rolled his eyes. “Donkey from Shrek. Onions, layers?”

“I have no idea what you’re talking about,” Del grumbled.

In unison, every eye turned to Del and Jake said, “I can’t believe you’ve got kids and have never heard of Shrek.”

Del grumbled under his breath. “Why would I watch a fuckin’ kids’ show?”

Ruiz clapped him on the shoulder. “You’ve got to get home more often, dude.”

“I need coffee.” Jake looked over to the counter. “Anyone else need anything?”

There was a rumble of, “We’re fine,” around the table, and he left them, feeling the momentary loss of Mitch’s closeness.

Jake smiled at the two women behind the counter. "Coffee please?"

The younger one, who was probably at least five years younger than Jake, studied him then her gaze flitted to the team. "You with them?"

"Yeah."

"Thought so." She looked at him, then back at them. "You look like them. Scary."

Jake chuckled. "Nah, we're all pussycats."

"More like tigers," she muttered, but she turned to pour the coffee.

The older woman winked at Jake. He grinned, making sure it was off his face when the young woman turned back. He took the coffee, smiled at them both and sat back down next to Mitch, who pressed in close.

"You've scored." Mitch's breath bathed his ear.

"Fuck off," Jake said easily and took a long swallow of coffee.

Mitch's hand slid up Jake's thigh. Jake couldn't repress his shiver.

"If you two have quite finished?" Lukas said acerbically.

Jake flushed but Mitch said nothing. If anything, he pressed closer.

Lukas huffed and tapped at his tablet. "Riley will be taken back to North Carolina as soon as he's well enough to travel. He'll go to the sheriff's office until they're here."

"Why? He's been exonerated," Ruiz insisted.

Lukas shook his head. "Of murder, yes, but we need a judge and the DA to agree. And he will be charged with escaping custody."

"But—"

Jake shook his head at Ruiz's protest and the man subsided. "What do we need to do? Does Riley need a lawyer?

I can do that." Riley was family... and Jake had put him in jail. Jake would sell the shirt off his back to get Riley where he belonged.

"It's already in process, but Riley will go back to jail until he's freed officially." Lukas looked around the table, his eyes stern. "You understand?" There was a low dissatisfied rumble but Lukas dragged a reluctant nod from everyone. "He won't be alone."

"He wasn't alone before," Ruiz said quietly and didn't that make Jake's stomach churn up in knots?

Mitch squeezed Jake's thigh as if he read Jake's thoughts. "What do you need us to do, Lukas?"

"You've got other things to worry about, Mitch." Lukas' eyes flickered to Jake. "And you've got a bar full of holes."

Jake grimaced at thought of the repairs. "Great. It's drafty enough without that."

"You should demolish the bar and start again," Mitch said.

Jake elbowed Mitch in answer to his sarcastic suggestion. "Hey, this is my home you're knocking."

Mitch yelped at Jake's sharp elbow, but he said, "The bar needs rebuilding from the ground up."

Jake growled but he knew Mitch was right. "Yeah, I know. Just never had enough money you know?"

Lukas frowned. "But what—"

Jake narrowed his eyes and Lukas shut up. Jake was aware of the curiosity from around the table, but he wasn't prepared to have *that* conversation. Not yet anyway.

To Jake's surprise, Mitch pushed Jake out of the booth. "Let's go relieve Si and Howie." He hustled Jake away from the team and out of the café. Once they were out of sight from everyone, Mitch shoved Jake up against the wall, just missing a notice board.

Jake flinched at the pain in his shoulder muscles as they hit the wall. “What the hell, Mitch?”

Mitch glared down at him, using his couple of inches extra height to his advantage. “You’re not short of money. You’ve got the half of our house when I bought you out, the money from Sharon’s insurance policy and from the sale of their house. Where’s all that money gone?”

“I don’t want to talk about it.” Jake turned his head, refusing to look at him.

“Jake...” Mitch gave a warning snarl, and reluctantly Jake caught his gaze.

He rested his hands lightly on Mitch’s hips. “The money from our house went to buying the bar.”

“And the rest?”

“It’s still in a bank account. I’ve not touched a cent.”

Mitch furrowed his brow. “I don’t understand.”

“I’m not sure I do either,” Jake admitted. “I thought about it. Heck knows I needed the money, but it just felt like blood money. Her blood.” Jake had felt dirty just thinking about it.

“What are you going to do with it now?”

“You mean Riley?” At Mitch’s nod, Jake sighed. “I’ll give it back to him. It’s his money, not mine.”

Mitch cupped Jake’s jaw with his large, warm hand and Jake couldn’t help leaning into the touch. “You’re amazing, Jacob Tyler. Do you know that?”

“Stupid, you mean.” Jake had thought he was stupid many times when he struggled to pay the bills every month. If it hadn’t been for Howie the bar would’ve gone under in the first year. Yet he still couldn’t bring himself to use the money.

“That’s not what I said.” Mitch’s eyes were warm and intense.

“You don’t need to.” Jake pressed a kiss to Mitch’s hand

and stepped away. "Let's get back to Riley before we get ourselves into trouble."

Mitch fell into step beside him as they walked down the hall. Jake brushed the back of Mitch's hand with his own. At least he had something concrete to offer Riley when he was released. Jake wondered when he'd stop feeling so damn guilty.

CHAPTER 14

In the days following the team's departure, Jake busied himself with repairing the bullet-ridden doors and walls. Each hole filled papered over the proof of the extraordinary week in the life of JT's Bar. His usual customers crowded the place, pleased, annoyed and with curiosity reeking from every pore at being kept out. Carl and Moose took them to see the bullet holes before Jake filled them and showed them where Marshall died. No one had any sympathy for the dead police officer.

Jake found himself exhausted and drained, struggling to get through each day and longing to fall into bed. But he hated going to bed alone. He'd had that one wonderful night with Mitch, but all it had done as remind him of how alone he'd been after his flight from Virginia.

He'd received a brief message from Mitch a few days after they'd left to say Riley had been transferred to a local hospital as he was running a fever. Jake was sure the sudden fever was the section's way of keeping him out of prison until the paperwork could be processed for his release. He would be charged with the escape but Lukas hoped to work out a deal with the District Attorney. Mitch said that Riley had also been promised his job back, if he wanted it. It wouldn't give him back his wife or the time he'd been locked up, but it was a start. Jake had sent Riley a private message to say he was welcome at JT's while he decided what he wanted to do next.

He hadn't heard anything but Si had told him Riley was thinking about it.

Mitch had called him once when he returned to Virginia, but other than that he'd only received a couple of messages, which had left Jake feeling depressed. He knew Mitch would be busy but he'd expected more than one call.

"You could call him, dumbass," he muttered to himself, but he knew he wouldn't.

It didn't help that Howie was wandering around the bar in blissful daze. Every time Jake turned around Howie was talking to Si, so yeah, maybe Jake was more than a little jealous. He knew Howie was thinking of making a permanent move to Virginia to be with him.

"You could move back too, dumbass. But what about Carl and the boys? They like the bar." Jake was getting real good at haranguing himself.

Three weeks after Mitch and the team went home, Jake still hadn't made any decisions, and Mitch had still only called him that once. He'd spoken to Del and Ruiz more than he had Mitch. Then Riley called him.

Jake grabbed the call like it was a lifeline. Riley was a connection to Mitch. "Hey, man. How are you?"

"Hey. I'm fine. I should be released soon. They're just thrashing out the plea deal."

Conversations between them were still awkward. Jake wasn't sure if Riley had forgiven him for getting him locked up for murder and he didn't like to ask. Si had assured Jake that Riley bore no ill-will, but Jake was unsure. He was convinced they would never get back to their previous relationship. But he would keep on hoping.

"What can I do for you?" Jake asked when the silence stretched on.

"I've made some decisions about my future."

"What are you going to do?"

"I'm going to retrain. Mitch said I can rejoin the team if I want to."

Jake wasn't sure Riley sounded convinced about his future plans. "Are you sure that's what you want?"

"I don't know, but I haven't got anything else to do." Riley sighed in his ear. "It's not going to be easy to find another job with my history."

"You know you're always welcome here." Jake would give Riley the shirt off his back if it would help.

"I don't think working in a bar is really my thing. But thanks for the offer. How are you doing?"

Jake was taken aback by the question. "I'm fine."

"No coughs, colds, headaches?"

Jake frowned, not sure where this was leading. "No."

"So why haven't you called Mitch?" Riley demanded.

"What?"

"He's waiting for your call, idiot."

Jake gritted his teeth. "He could call me."

Riley snorted in his ear. "What are you? Five? Call the man. He's falling apart."

"How do you know?"

"He visits me every couple of days."

Jake took a shaky breath. "He does?"

"Yeah. All the team do."

The guilt in Jake's gut churned away at him. "Riley—"

"It's okay, Jake," Riley said soothingly. "You're thousands of miles away and you've got a business to run."

"I'll be there when you get out. I promise." If Jake had to run to North Carolina he would be there.

"I know you will." The confidence in Riley's voice helped. Jake heard people talking at the other end and Riley said, "Damn. Sorry, I've got to go." He disconnected before Jake could say goodbye.

Jake stared at the phone for a long while. He'd got an ass-chewing, which he deserved. What the hell was he going to do about it?

Despite that conversation, it took Jake several days to call Mitch which, of course, went straight to voicemail. When he spoke to Howie he discovered the team were on another op and not expected back for a couple of months. So, there was Jake, on the outside.

Carl caught Jake by the restrooms. "You need this?" He handed Jake a green and blue toothbrush.

Jake stared at him, not having a clue what Carl was talking about. "Huh?"

"You break rule number 1, you do the punishment."

Jake frowned. "I haven't broken rule number 1"

"What is rule number 1?" Carl said.

"What're you talking about?"

"Just say it."

Jake huffed but he decided to humor him. "Mitch's word is fucking law. There is no other fucking law except Mitch's. And if you fucking forget Mitch rules the goddamn world you'll be cleaning the latrines for a fucking week. With a toothbrush."

"You broke the rule, you clean the latrines."

Jake shook his head. "Carl, I clean the restrooms every day. And what's Mitch got to do with it?"

"If he rules the goddamn world, why're you still here?"

"Carl, have you been at the Jack already? I own this bar, remember? Mitch works in Virginia. Besides, I haven't heard from him since he left."

"You're an idiot, Jake Tyler." Carl rapped on Jake's forehead with his knuckles.

Jake rubbed his now sore head. "What the fuck did you do that for?"

"He's waiting for you to go after him." Carl's tone suggested Mitch was obviously lacking if he wanted Jake.

"What? No, he's not."

"Jake, you musta been standing at the back of the line when they gave out sense. Don't you get it?"

Jake obviously didn't get it or he'd not be floundering in a conversation he didn't understand. "You explain it to me."

"You walked out on Mitch. Now you've got to go get him back. He won't come after you. He's too afraid of rejection."

"Carl, I can't go running across the country. I've got the bar to run. Besides, they're on an op. I've no idea when they'll be back."

"You don't think Howie will know the second they're back? The only reason he hasn't gone already is they got sent out. I can run the bar while you're gone. Me, Moose and Doug."

Jake looked at Carl like he'd lost his mind. "The three of you? Do you remember what Moose is like in the kitchen?"

Carl flapped his hand impatiently. "I can do the chow. You don't need to worry about that."

"I don't know." The thought of leaving his bar in Moose's hands didn't inspire Jake with a great deal of confidence.

"Yeah, you do. I'm telling you, when Howie tells you they're back you get on a plane and make nice with your boy."

Jake frowned at him. "Will I have a bar when I get back?"

"The bar and its customers have been here longer than you, son. It'll survive without you for a few days."

Jake stared at him dubiously. "If you're sure."

"I'm sure. Now you insist Howie tells you when they're back."

Six weeks later Jake found himself on a flight to Washington with Howie next to him. Jake had gladly given up the window seat. This was Howie's first flight and between his excitement at being on a plane and the thought of seeing Si again, he was almost rattling beside Jake.

Jake had already taken one trip across the countryside to greet Riley when he was released from prison and take him to retraining. This trip was different. Mitch didn't know Jake was coming. Jake had sworn Si to secrecy. He didn't want Mitch to feel obliged to do anything. If he turned up and Mitch looked horrified, Jake would just get the next flight back to Wyoming. He could live with the rejection. At least that's what he kept telling himself.

At the airport, Howie virtually leapt into Si's arms. If they were going for manly hugs and thumps on the back they missed by a mile. Jake stood guard, ready to take down anyone who tried to ruin their happiness, but no one paid them any attention, too busy going about their business.

Finally, Howie unwrapped his arms from around Si's neck, giving Jake an opportunity to greet his friend, who studied him closely.

"You look like shit," Si declared.

Jake saluted him. "Thanks."

"You're welcome. Your boy does, too. He's been a miserable asshole since we got back." Si winked. "That's your fault by the way."

Jake didn't bother to protest. Everyone was telling him the same thing.

Si led the way to his old truck. Jake gladly relinquished the front seat to Howie, as it left him a chance to think. Si drove them through the evening traffic while carrying on an animated discussion with Howie. Deep in thought, Jake hadn't paid attention to where Si was going. A sudden jolt disturbed his thoughts and Jake looked up to discover that, instead of Si's place, they were outside his old home in Woodbridge.

"I thought we were going to your place?" Jake said, his stomach churning.

Si looked over his shoulder. "No time like the present. Besides, you didn't travel three thousand miles just to listen to me and Howie fuck, did you?"

Howie blushed deep red. "Si!"

Jake just rolled his eyes and got out of the truck. Si was right, this was what he was here for. Jake needed to grab his balls and go talk to Mitch. Or talk to Mitch and grab Mitch's balls.

Si left him standing on the sidewalk. Jake didn't know what he was going to do if Mitch told him to fuck off. Find a cab to take him back to the airport, he guessed. He hoisted his small backpack and turned to look at his old home. Nothing had changed. By the door the geraniums still spilled haphazardly out of the pots he and Mitch had chosen together, and the house was still the same shade of pale blue that upset the neighbors. Jake didn't know how long he'd stood there but, before he took a step, the front door opened and Mitch stared at him, a shocked expression on his face.

"Jake?"

"Hi." Jake stayed where he was, not sure if he was going to be invited in.

Mitch didn't look as though he'd decided about that either. Jake studied him carefully. Si had been right about one thing. He looked like crap. He was obviously tired; Jake could see that by the dark smudges under his eyes and the tight lines around his mouth, and he'd lost weight in the two months since Jake had last seen him. He was shirtless, wearing only low-cut faded jeans that rode low on his hips, a perfect frame for his muscled form and his feet were bare. Mitch wearing jeans and nothing else had always been a turn on for Jake, but his ribs were too pronounced and he bordered on skinny.

"You're not eating," Jake said.

Mitch shrugged. "I haven't felt hungry lately."

They stared at each other, the silence stretching into awkwardness, until Mitch said, "Are you coming in?"

It wasn't the enthusiastic reception Jake had hoped for but it was probably better than he deserved. Mitch stood back to let Jake into the house. The breath caught in Jake's throat as he walked inside. The place even smelled the same; a mixture of lavender, pizza and musk. Jake could've just stepped out for a beer.

Mitch still didn't look that enthused to see Jake. "Why're you here?"

Jake bit his lip. He'd gone over what he was going to say time and again, but all the words vanished as he gazed at Mitch. Finally, he managed to stutter out, "T-To see you."

"Why?" Mitch asked bluntly.

Jake tried again. "You didn't call me."

"You didn't call *me*."

At this rate, they'd be exchanging terse sentences until Jake had to go home. Jake decided direct action was better. He wrapped a hand around Mitch's neck, hauled him closer and pulled him down for a kiss. Mitch resisted for a few seconds, then he groaned and suddenly he was the one in control. Jake let him take over. He didn't care who was kissing who, as long as it didn't stop. Jake tangled his fingers into the loops of Mitch's jeans to pull him even closer, his knuckles grazing Mitch's cool skin. Mitch squirmed a little and Jake grinned, remembering how ticklish he was.

Their kisses changed; less angry and frantic, more heated

and needy. The scruff of late afternoon shadow rasped Jake's cheeks but he didn't care. It was a welcome pain, triggering other memories of kisses stolen in deep shadows. Mitch moaned again and Jake captured the sound. They stumbled as Jake tripped over one of Mitch's feet. The easy rhythm of the past wasn't there.

Mitch pulled back. "I've got to—"

"Yes." Jake agreed.

"You—"

"Yes." Jake didn't know what he was agreeing to as long as it involved him, skin, and being fucked senseless.

Mitch snorted as if he knew Jake didn't have a clue, then he dragged Jake up the stairs but, instead of turning left to the master bedroom, he turned right into what had been their guest room. Jake frowned. As if Mitch read his mind he said, "I couldn't sleep in there once you left."

Jake nodded. He needed to process that later, but not now. Now he needed to hang onto the headboard while Mitch fucked him into next week.

Without any finesse, they stripped off their clothes. Jake could put on a show later. Now he just wanted skin on skin. Mitch only had his jeans to take off and Jake didn't fail to notice he'd been going commando. Jake's jacket went flying, swiftly followed by his shirt and undershirt. Mitch tried to help, but Jake batted his hands away when he became more of a hindrance.

Jake shoved down his jeans and briefs, only to discover he'd made the fatal error of undressing while in lust. "Fuck, my boots."

Mitch dealt with it by shoving Jake backwards onto the bed and pulling off Jake's boots for him. Then he threw himself on top of Jake and, fucking finally, the world was right again. For the first time in too long Jake was where he should be. Under Mitch, naked with Mitch, and with Mitch's teeth sunk into his neck. Jake pushed himself into that pain, needing more, needing to be reminded of his place. They'd never had the Top/bottom, Dom/sub, relationship. Jake liked fucking Mitch just as much as Mitch liked fucking Jake. They followed each other's lead and this was what Jake wanted now. He wriggled until he could wrap his legs around Mitch.

Mitch raised his head. "I can't make this smooth and romantic. Not this time. You've got to let me—"

"Do it!" Jake growled.

Mitch reached over and pulled open the drawer of the nightstand for condoms and lube. He fumbled with the lube. Jake took it from him and squirted some on Mitch's fingers then he laid back, legs open, a blatant invitation to get the hell on with the show. Mitch paused for a moment, his heated gaze a hot caress over Jake's body. Then, as Jake reached for him, Mitch leaned over and slid a finger into Jake, then another and it burned, but Jake took it, welcomed it. Then fingers weren't enough. He needed Mitch inside him. Jake fumbled for the condom. Between them they rolled the rubber down Mitch's cock and slathered it with lube, then Mitch pushed Jake back onto the pillows and he entered Jake's body. Jake gasped; it had been a while, but despite Mitch's obvious urgency, he took his time, pushing in slowly, little rocks of his hips easing the way. Mitch took Jake's moans and returned them with his own. They didn't part their mouths until Mitch was fully seated inside Jake. He closed his eyes as Mitch pushed in the last half inch. He was home, finally home.

"I'm home." Mitch sounded awed.

Jake opened his eyes and stared into Mitch's dark blue depths. "You *are* home."

Mitch nodded. "*You're* my home." Then he rocked again and Jake clutched at his shoulders. Mitch pulled out until the head of his cock stretched Jake wide.

"Come on, come on," Jake begged.

Mitch pushed back in until he was enfolded by Jake's body. Fast this time and Jake groaned loudly. "Too much?" Mitch asked.

"Not fucking enough," Jake growled, digging his fingers into Mitch's hips.

Mitch opened his mouth to retort, but Jake hauled him down for another kiss. Mitch could do better things with his mouth than talk. Mitch kissed him fiercely, teeth clashing, whiskers rasping, tongues dueling until Jake felt the tension building inside of him. He needed more. He thrust up, demanding more. Mitch fucked him steadily, the rhythm building, catching, until they were growling and grunting at each other. They were noisy, messy, Jake's dick leaking more with every thrust. Then Mitch faltered, thrust again and came with a shout, pulsing into the condom. Jake went to jerk himself off to reach his own climax, but Mitch batted his hand away, pulled out and bent to suck Jake into a warm, wet cavern. It took a few hard sucks and Jake pulsed down Mitch's throat.

Mitch licked Jake clean then he released him, disposed of the condom and crawled up the bed until he lay next to Jake. Jake turned onto his side to face him, one hand resting on Mitch's thigh. Mitch looked... happy. Still tired, still too thin, but happy.

"Why did you take so long to come here?" Mitch asked.

Jake could've pointed out that he wasn't the one who'd disappeared for nearly two months, but instead he was honest. "I didn't know that's what I was supposed to do. Carl was the one who kicked my butt and told me to get here."

"You always were oblivious."

"Yeah."

Mitch smiled and Jake's heart did a pitter-patter as he returned the smile. "Are you staying?"

Jake frowned. "You know I can't. The bar..."

The smile slid off Mitch's face. "Then why are you here?"

"To see you."

"*This* is your home, Jake. Not the bar."

Jake sat up and wrapped his arms around his knees. "Not any more it isn't. I'm not in ops now. I own the bar, I can't just run away from it. It would be like me asking you to be a barman."

"Why don't you?" Mitch said.

"What?" Jake turned to look down at him.

"Give me a job."

"You're a leader of a covert ops team, not a barman."

"So were you."

Mitch seemed deadly serious so Jake did as he asked. "Okay. Mitch Mitchelson, would you come live with me in bumfuck Wyoming and be my alpha barman?"

"Yes."

CHAPTER 15

"What?"

Mitch chuckled at Jake's wide-eyed stare. "I said yes. When do I start?"

"But you... your job..." Jake wondered if he was dreaming but Mitch just shrugged.

"I resigned before I left. I'm now unemployed. You willing to take me on?"

"You're fuckin' crazy!" Jake knelt and glared down at him. "What the hell did you do that for?"

Mitch frowned. He sat up and thumped a pillow into shape, nesting it, then himself against the headboard before he spoke again. "Why're you so angry?"

"I'm not angry, asshole." Jake clenched his fists. He wasn't angry, he was fucking livid. What the hell did Mitch think he was doing?

"Isn't this what you want?" Mitch asked. "You and me together? Don't tell me it's not what you want."

"Of course I want this." Jake was vibrating with anger. He wanted to shake the living shit out of Mitch. "But you giving up your whole life for me? That's not right."

Mitch shook his head. "I'm not doing this for you, Jake. I'm doing it for me. I'm getting old."

"You're almost the same age as me, dipshit. You've got another five years easy."

"I've been in ops for eight years now and too much has

happened. I'm burned out, Jake."

Jake pressed his lips together. "But—"

"Shut up, Jake." Mitch leaned forward and placed a finger over Jake's mouth. "If you hadn't come here today, I would've been on the next flight to Wyoming. You're not the only one who's been moping around. Si and Riley threatened to kick my ass all the way back to the bar if I didn't do something."

"Maybe Carl and Si have been talking."

"Maybe." Mitch didn't sound as if he cared much. "If we hadn't got this last op I would have been with you weeks ago. You're frowning again. What's the matter now?"

"I don't think the bar can support you as well as me and Howie. You've seen the state of the place. We're scraping by as it is."

"Have you spoken to Howie?"

"No. Why is there something you know that I don't?"

"He wants to move here to be with Si. I don't think he'd object to me buying him out of JT's."

"Okay." Jake pressed his lips together. He'd expected something like it for weeks. "O-kay."

"You sound like you don't approve."

"It's not disapproval. I just wonder if they're rushing it. I'm worried about Howie. He doesn't have much experience with guys. What happens if he gets here and they both find it's been a huge mistake? He's going to have to find a job, and Si will be away for weeks at a time."

"Howie's a big boy and Si's a good man. They'll sort it out between them." Mitch shot Jake a shrewd look. "Or are you jealous now Howie's found someone else?"

"No." Jake stopped a moment. "*No!* Well..., maybe a little."

"Don't worry. I'll keep you fully occupied."

Jake rolled his eyes. “Can we just not rush with the buyout? I don’t want Howie to end up short of money.”

Mitch shrugged. “I’m in no rush. All I want…,” he dragged Jake so that he was straddling Mitch’s thighs, “is to be with you. I don’t care whether I’m your employee, partner or intern. I’ve got enough money to support both of us for a while.”

Jake leaned his hands against Mitch’s furred chest, his thumbs brushing Mitch’s dark nipples. “I never did find out how you managed to buy me out. I thought you just got a bigger mortgage.”

“My grandmother died. She left me some money.”

“I’m sorry. She was a lovely woman,” Jake said.

“No, she wasn’t. She was an old bitch, as well you know.” Mitch gave a rueful smile. “She hated the fact that I was gay, but she still loved me.”

Jake remembered the uncomfortable visits to Mitch’s paternal grandmother. Susan Mitchelson never made Jake feel welcome, but he accepted it because it was obvious how much she loved Mitch. They’d formed an uneasy bond through their mutual love for him. “And you loved her.”

Mitch nodded. “For all her faults, yeah, I did. And she left me enough money to buy you out initially, and enough to help you now.”

“She would’ve hated that.” Jake and Mitch smirked at each other as they imagined what her reaction would have been.

Then Mitch leaned forward and kissed him. “I love you, Jake. I never stopped loving you. And you really don’t want to live here, do you?”

Jake shook his head. “I’m not going back to the team.”

“Riley’ll be disappointed. I think he’s been hoping you would.”

"I thought about it," Jake admitted. "But I've been out too long."

"Riley's been away just as long."

"I know. But he's always loved the thrill of the action."

"You didn't?" Mitch stroked Jake's arms, the gesture soothing Jake's jangled nerves.

"I did at first. I wouldn't have joined the team otherwise."

"But your feelings changed?

Jake nodded slowly. "I think so. I loved working with the team. I loved working with you. But I didn't need the thrills from doing the assignments. I just needed you."

"And now all I need is you."

Mitch cupped a hand around Jake's head, tugged him closer and kissed him. Jake closed his eyes and accepted Mitch's mouth on his, parting his lips at Mitch's urging. Their tongues dueled lazily as Mitch put his arms around Jake and held him tightly. Jake sunk into the feeling of Mitch around him, soft skin overlaying hard muscle and the friction of hair all adding to the sensation. Jake ran his fingers through Mitch's soft fuzz and held his head just so, focusing on the kiss. Eventually Mitch sighed and settled them into a more comfortable position, stroking Jake's hair. Jake laid his head against Mitch's neck, his mouth just resting against his rough skin.

"Are you sure about working for me?" Jake said after a long while.

"If it doesn't work out then I can find another job. It's no big deal. We've lived and worked together before. It worked then."

Jake grunted.

Mitch snorted. "You're such a doubter."

Jake laid one hand over Mitch's heart. "Just scared."

Mitch placed his large hand over Jake's. "You don't need

to be. I'm moving to Wyoming and nothing's going to stop us."

"Dude, do you want to jinx us?"

"What?" Mitch sounded confused.

Jake raised his head to look at Mitch. "Have you never watched a movie? The minute a couple declares their love and says they're going to be together forever, one of them dies. It always happens."

"That's the movies. This is real-life. We're gonna be fine." Mitch patted Jake's hand. "Do you want food? I'm starving." Jake hadn't thought about being hungry until Mitch mentioned it but his stomach growled in anticipation. "I'll take that as a yes."

"Take-out?"

Mitch pulled a face. "I've eaten too much take-out lately."

"You look as though you haven't eaten anything." Jake ran a finger over Mitch's prominent ribs.

"I lost interest in food. Now though, I could eat a horse. Pancakes and bacon?" Mitch climbed off the bed and scratched his belly.

Jake took time to admire Mitch. He was totally edible. "Sounds great. Want me to cook?"

He expected Mitch to leap at the chance. One of the few bones of contention between them had been because Jake did most of the cooking. To his surprise, Mitch shook his head.

"Let's cook together."

"Sure."

Jake followed Mitch's example and slipped on jeans and a T-shirt. He trotted downstairs in bare feet. Nothing much had changed in the kitchen, and they worked side by side without any hesitation. After a while they sat at the breakfast bar with a stack of pancakes, bacon and coffee.

After another stack and more bacon than was good for him, Jake groaned and sat back, rubbing his stomach. “That was so good.”

Mitch shoved the last piece of bacon in his mouth and echoed, “*So* good.”

Jake drank his coffee, remembering the hours he and Mitch had spent in this kitchen; reading books and playing games, fresh hot coffee always available. Back home he tended to drink sweet tea because he always had a jug in the fridge.

“When do we have to go back?” Mitch said suddenly.

Jake’s heart jumped at the ‘we’. “I ought to be back by the end of the week.”

“I’ll pack up the house and get movers organized. Say I’ll be with you by the end of the month... and if you say, ‘are you sure’ one more time I’ll gag you.” Jake shut his mouth without a word. Mitch nodded in satisfaction. “You need to talk to Howie, and I need to talk to my parents.” He pulled a face and Jake smirked.

“Your dad’s going to go nuts.”

“Don’t remind me,” Mitch groaned.

“Covert ops leader to barman. He’s not gonna be happy.”

“I said, don’t remind me,” Mitch growled but he had a smile playing about his lips.

“Your mom’ll be pleased.”

“At least I’m not likely to be shot at on a daily basis.”

Jake gave him an incredulous look. “Mitch, you have met my customers, right? Most of them are packing. Why do you think I don’t redecorate?”

“At least they won’t be aiming at me,” Mitch amended.

“Just wait ‘til Moose and Doug get into it when they’ve had a few too many. You have to duck.”

Mitch rolled his eyes. “I probably won’t tell Mom that.”

"Wise move." Jake frowned as he heard music. "Is that your phone?"

"Yeah. Must be Lukas." Mitch stood and reached over to the dresser to pick up his phone. "Hey, Lukas."

Jake got up to pour himself another coffee. When he turned back to the table he saw the rigid look on Mitch's face. "What's happened?"

Mitch held up his hand as he listened to Lukas. "Is he okay? Don't let him out of your sight. Yeah, I got weapons."

Weapons? What the hell? Jake waited impatiently for Mitch to end his conversation.

"Get them here. If he's gone after Riley, the next target is Jake. Have you notified the police? Make sure you let them know we're here."

"What the fuck's going on?"

Mitch shook his head. "Wait."

Jake was on the brink of telling Mitch what he could do with his order when Mitch put the phone down. "Someone took a potshot at Riley at the training ground."

"What? Is he okay?"

"He's fine. He moved and the bullet grazed his shoulder. But another trainee was hit. He's in a critical condition."

"Shit."

"Who the hell's after Riley?" If Jake hadn't been watching Mitch closely he would've missed the tic under his eye twitch. "Don't you think of lyin' to me." At Mitch's silence, Jake slammed his hand down on the counter. Coffee spilled from the refilled mugs. "Mitch!"

"The police think… they know Marshall and Sanchez had a third partner in their burglary operation."

"Do they know who it is?" Jake demanded.

Mitch shook his head. "The detectives had their suspicions but no proof."

"Is it one of them. Another dirty cop?"

"Yeah," Mitch said. "But it was all just circumstantial evidence and not enough to hold him on."

"Who was it?"

"Marshall's brother, Rick."

"He's a cop?"

"He was. Got kicked off the force six months ago although Lukas can't find out why. From what I hear he was a ticking time-bomb."

"And Marshall's death lit the fuse?"

Mitch nodded, his expression tight. "Looks like it. Lukas wanted to warn us. He could be on the way here."

"Fuck," Jake muttered, "didn't we just do this?"

Mitch gulped down the last of his coffee. "I've got two Glocks in the safe."

"'Kay." Jake finished his drink and put the mugs in the sink. He wasn't ready for another confrontation. Mitch came behind him and squeezed his shoulder.

"It's all right, Jake. Del and Ruiz are on their way. Si's taking care of Riley and Howie. We'll get the bastard."

Jake gripped the edge of the sink. "We'd better. This better be the last Marshall sibling or I'm gonna get real pissed off."

"Stay away from the windows."

Jake looked over his shoulder at Mitch. "You didn't just say that."

Mitch's lips twitched. "You're right. I didn't. I wouldn't be that stupid." He stepped back and headed to the gun safe before he got himself into more trouble.

Jake took the old Glock Mitch handed him. He'd used one in practice when they were together, so he was familiar with it. They loaded the guns and retreated to the bedroom to dress in hoodies and put on socks and boots. Jake didn't want to get caught barefoot.

Mitch's phone rang again. Jake answered it as Mitch was putting on his boots.

"Jake here."

"Hey Jake, it's Del."

"Del," he mouthed to Mitch. "Hey."

"We're five minutes out. You armed?"

"Yes. Be careful coming in."

The offended silence told Jake he'd just done the exact same thing Mitch had pulled on him. "I'm sorry. I'm jumpy."

"Nearly there." Del disconnected the call abruptly.

Mitch snickered. "He didn't appreciate you stating the obvious?"

"Something like that," Jake muttered.

Mitch looked as if he was about to laugh when suddenly his expression changed. "Old Mr. Farman's dogs are barking."

Jake nodded. The two German Shepherds only barked when people got too close to their property. Most of the locals knew to avoid Farman's yard. The barking cut off abruptly on a muffled howl and Mitch's eyes opened wide at the realization of what that meant.

"Fucking bastard."

Jake knew Mitch had a fondness for the dogs despite their noise. With that one act Rick Marshall was a dead man walking. "I didn't hear the shots."

"He's using a silencer. I'm going to kill him."

"You do that, lover. Just don't get yourself shot in the process."

Mitch shot him a fierce grin. "You're on."

They went through the house making sure all the doors and windows were locked, all except one. Jake and Mitch didn't want to deter him from entering the house. They just wanted him to do it on their terms.

The door handle squeaked as it was turned. Jake rolled his eyes. It had squeaked when Jake lived there. He heard the hushed *pad pad pad* of rubber-soled shoes over the tiled floor in the laundry room. The room was too narrow to ambush Rick Marshall but all he had to do was take one step out of the—

"Stay the fuck where you are," Mitch ordered.

Rick Marshall froze.

"Place your weapons on the floor."

From Jake's position, he watched Rick hesitate, obviously considering his options. Perhaps he needed the order reinforced. "You heard what he said," Jake growled.

Rick hesitated and Jake could tell the exact moment he made his decision. As if in slow-motion Rick brought up his rifle in Mitch's direction and Jake didn't hesitate. One shot. Rick's legs collapsed underneath him and he fell to the floor.

Mitch approached him cautiously and kicked away the rifle. Jake removed the gun from the leg holster.

A noise behind Jake and he swung around, weapon ready, but it was Del.

"Is he dead?" Del asked.

Mitch nudged Rick with his toe. "He's making a good attempt at it."

"You could've waited," Del complained. "I missed my kid's birthday party for this."

Jake snorted. "You wanna go back?"

"Are you stupid? There are twenty eight-year-old girls in the family room." Del whined like one of his kids. "They all want to braid hair and talk about who Taylor Swift is dating. It's hell."

"I'm sure I can find you something to do," Mitch promised. "I've got to see Farman about his dogs."

Jake ignored the man on the floor. “I’ll come with you. Del and Ruiz can deal with Marshall. Shit, there aren’t any other brothers, are there?”

“There’d better not be,” Del said grimly. “I’ll kill ‘em now to save time.”

Ruiz stepped into the laundry room. “Finished?” He barely glanced at Marshall. “The cops are here.”

“They can take him. He’s one of theirs.” Jake looked at Mitch. “Let’s deal with Farman.”

Mitch grunted in agreement and they escaped out the back before they could be stopped by police officers gathering in front of the house.

Farman lived two lots over and they found the old man in the yard, kneeling by the two large German Shepherds lying in the dirt. He looked up, tears running down his cheeks. Jake swallowed the lump in his throat at the naked grief in the old man’s wrinkled face.

“I’m so sorry, Mr. Farman.” Mitch knelt by his neighbor and placed a hand on his shoulder.

“But why? Why did he hurt my boys?” Farman was shocked and bewildered.

“He knew their barking would alert me.”

“Tell me you killed him.” Farman glared at Mitch fiercely.

“Jake did.”

“Good.” Farman looked up then, and he blinked as he recognized Jake. “Didn’t expect to see you again, son.”

Jake knelt beside them. Poor pups. Then he looked closer. *Holy shit!* “They’re still alive!” Although he didn’t know how long for.

The dark-furred dog nearest to them was taking shallow breaths. Mr. Farman stroked the dog’s head and the dog gave a weak thump of his tail. The other one was also breathing—just.

"Sammy!" Mr. Farman's voice cracked. "Deano!"

"What?" Mitch said. "Where's your vet, Mr. Farman?"

"Near IKEA. But I couldn't afford the insurance." Farman's lip wobbled.

"We'll settle this," Mitch said. "I need blankets for them."

Jake helped Mr. Farman to his feet and watched him limp slowly into his house. He looked at Mitch. "Do you think we can save them?"

Mitch stroked the dogs, making soothing, crooning noises. One of them gave a small whine. "Who knows, but I'm not giving up on them. Get Ruiz ready with the car."

Jake rushed back to the house, pushing past the police officers. "Ruiz, Ruiz!"

Ruiz looked up, a startled look on his face. "What's wrong?"

"You need to take Mitch to the vet." Jake held up his hand as Ruiz's eyes lit up. "Save the jokes for later. There are two shot dogs out there."

One of the police officers, who looked as if he was going to stop Ruiz, stepped forward. "I'll drive them."

Jake took him back to Mitch and Mr. Farman. Between them they got the dogs settled in the back of the police cruiser and it screeched off, lights flashing.

Jake put his arm around Mr. Farman. "I'd take you back to Mitch's place but it's a crime scene at the moment."

The old man gave a shaky laugh. "It's all right, son. I'll wait to hear from your young man." Jake stared at him, wide-eyed and Mr. Farman laughed again. "You think I didn't know?"

"I...." Jake shook his head.

"Mitch spent a lot of time with me after you left. When he wasn't off saving the world." Mr. Farman patted Jake's arm. "He missed you, young man."

"You don't mind?"

"Maybe once I might have. Now it's none of my business. I'm just happy to see you here." Mr. Farman's voice broke again as he looked at the two blood-stained circles of dirt in his yard. "No one should be alone. You're old a long time. You need all the friends you can get."

Jake nodded. "I know. Let me make you a drink."

He guided Mr. Farman back into his shabby house and sent up a prayer for Sammy and Deano, hoping their lives wouldn't be snuffed out by a senseless act.

EPILOGUE

Two months later

The lack of conversation in the bar should have alerted Jake, but it had been proven before that he was oblivious when it came to noticing things like that.

Howie nudged him. "They're here."

"Who?" Jake looked at him, confused.

Howie rolled his eyes. "Who do you think?"

A smile broke over Jake's face as he looked up to see the team sitting at their favorite table. Si waved and nudged Riley, who looked up and gave Jake a salute.

Jake saluted back, pleased Riley looked a lot better than the last time he'd seen him, which had been a couple of hours after being shot by Rick Marshall.

"Mitch, they're here!" Jake yelled into the private area at the back of the bar.

He heard the *thump thump thump* of heavy boots and Mitch appeared, his face lit up with excitement. Jake nodded toward the table and Mitch headed over there, Jake hard on his heels. The team got up and there was an orgy of hugging and thumping of backs as they greeted each other. Jake was sure he heard Del muttering how much he missed Mitch into his neck.

Si hugged Mitch, cursing him up and down for leaving them. Then he turned to Jake. "How are you?"

"I'm fine. Go on." Jake held him tightly and thumped his back twice. "Talk to your boy."

Si laughed and headed eagerly over to Howie. They met

with a clash of muscle and searching hands. The couple had been separated for two months and Jake knew how hard it had been on them. Howie had spent hours on the phone to Si between the team's assignments. Jake had learned to disappear during those times, as shy Howie had quite the turn of phrase when it came to expressing his feelings. Jake had told him, much to Howie's embarrassment, he'd have made a fortune as a phone sex operator.

"Put him down!" Moose yelled from the corner of the bar.

"Which one?" Carl said.

"Both. Look at 'em. Jeez. Find a room." Moose was grumbling but he didn't sound that bothered.

Howie flipped the bird vaguely in Moose's direction, not even bothering to raise his head. There was a shocked silence in the bar then everyone burst out laughing. Howie never flipped anyone off, not even Jake. As the whistling began, Jake hoped his floor would stand up to the stomping of boots. Si ignored them all and pushed Howie in the direction of the back.

"Stay outta the bedroom," Jake shouted after them. He didn't hold up much hope that either of them would pay any attention. There were fresh sheets on the bed and clean sheets waiting in the closet. Mitch was good like that.

Jake went behind the bar and brought back beers for everyone. Del reached eagerly for a bottle and chugged back half the contents before putting it down.

"Damn, I needed that."

Jake raised an eyebrow. "Bad day?"

"Del's had a bit of a shock," Ruiz told him. "His wife's just told him she's pregnant."

Mitch whistled. "You're gonna be a daddy again? Congratulations!"

Del looked at him sourly. "Did you have to say that?"

Mitch furrowed his brow, obviously confused. “What?”

“The D word.” Del finished the rest of the bottle. He held it out to Jake. “Keep ‘em coming.”

“Ooh, it really is bad.” Jake went to get up but Mitch pushed him down.

“Stay there. I’ll get another round.” He smiled at Jake and went behind the bar.

Jake stared after him, admiring his tight ass for a few moments. He turned his attention back to the group and caught Riley watching him, a sad smile playing around his lips, pain in his eyes. “Are you okay?”

“Yes.” The answer was too quick and Jake just waited. “No, I’m not.” Riley sighed heavily. “But I will be. It’ll take a while to get over being incarcerated. It’s *okay*, Jake.”

Jake had flinched at his words. “But it’s not okay, is it?”

Riley leaned forward. “I have my life back now, although I miss Sharon. At least I have somewhere to live. If you hadn’t put the money in trust I’d be homeless.”

Riley had taken over Mitch’s house until he made plans of his own. Mitch had made him promise faithfully to keep an eye on Mr. Farman and the two dogs. Miraculously, both dogs had survived, although Deano was taking much longer to recover. One good thing was they were much quieter now.

“You’d never be homeless,” Ruiz said. “You could’ve lived with Del and the kids.” Del shoved Ruiz and it was only his quick reflexes that stopped him tumbling on the floor. Ruiz recovered his balance and shoved Del back. “Ass!”

“Settle down or you’ll spill the beer,” Mitch warned as he came back with five more bottles. “Moose, you’re behind the bar.”

Moose saluted. “Yes, sir.”

Ruiz raised another bottle. “Look at you. I never thought our big bad leader would end up as a barman and you’re still running the show."

Jake thought he ought to be offended by that but Mitch's smile was huge. He settled next to Jake and stroked his thigh.

"I can't believe you've settled down," Del said.

Mitch wrapped an arm around Jake's shoulders. "I'm very happy working for Jake."

Jake hooted derisively. "Working *for* me? Dude, you've never worked *for* me in your life."

"He's still pushing you around?" Ruiz asked.

Jake winked at Mitch. "I don't mind." He laughed as Ruiz and Del made gagging sounds.

"Dude, I don't need to know that." Ruiz grabbed his bottle and drank as if clearing a bad taste in his mouth.

Mitch wrapped his arms around Jake and nuzzled his neck. "I push him around just enough. But he's the boss."

"Aw, you are such a pretty liar." Jake tilted his head so he could kiss Mitch. "He's not lying about pushing me around though."

Mitch tugged Jake against him and Jake settled back happily, reveling in the feel of the hard chest against his back. He drank his beer and watched as the team caught up with the gossip. Riley hadn't recovered his natural exuberance but he was getting there.

After a while Si and Howie joined them. Howie was a little hesitant but Si pulled him down and gave him a sloppy kiss on the cheek.

Jake watched his team talk excitedly to Mitch, telling him as much as they could about their last assignments. He couldn't help the niggle of worry. Would Mitch be content here, in the middle of nowhere? He was an action man, not a barman.

"Stop worrying," Mitch murmured. "I can hear you thinking from here."

"You're not a mind-reader," Jake protested.

"I'm not wishing I was back on the team."

"Maybe you are," Jake muttered. He sighed and nuzzled into Mitch. "Are you sure?"

"I'm sure. I'd been thinking of retiring for over a year. I already told you that. I'm happy here, Jake. I'm with you. That's all I need." Mitch tightened his arm around Jake and, although Jake made a token protest about spilling his beer, he settled back, soothed by Mitch's reassurance.

"So, when's Howie leaving?" Del asked after a while.

Si beamed widely. "Beginning of the month. We're buying a new place together not far from Riley's. We'll make sure Riley doesn't trash the place with his wild parties."

Riley groaned. "You're gonna cramp my style with the ladies, man." But he winked at Howie and laughed, and Jake already knew he was pleased someone was looking out for him.

"Wild parties? Hey, I'm missing out," Mitch protested.

Jake snorted. "We have wild parties here. Only last week."

"That was Brad and his posse getting liquored up and Mitch throwing them out," Howie pointed out.

"Oh yeah, so he did." Jake grinned at Mitch. "My alpha barman."

The patrons of JT's had learned to their cost that if Jake had their backs, Mitch was there for Jake. When Jake tried to break up a fight and Brad threw a punch, Mitch was there immediately, throwing them out of the bar before they had a chance to argue. Jake had said nothing until later when he'd shown Mitch with his mouth, hands and eager cock, just how happy he was to have him there at his side.

Ruiz banged his fist on the table, making all the bottles jump. "We can start the wild party now!"

"Dude, mind my beer," Si grumbled as his bottle wobbled

dangerously.

Jake leaned back against Mitch, feeling the warmth of his hand bleed through his shirt. The team was together again, if only for a night of booze and reminiscing.

"You okay?" Mitch's low question brushed his ear.

"I'm fine. What about you?"

"Haven't we just had this conversation?" Mitch growled. "I like talking about old times, but that's what they are. Old times. What I like more is waking up next to you, rolling you over and sliding into your tight—"

"Not here!" Jake slapped a hand over Mitch's mouth so he couldn't continue. Mitch's eyes twinkled devilishly over Jake's hand.

"Yeah, not here, Mitch." Si threw a cashew at Jake, who plucked it out of the air and tossed it into his mouth.

Mitch snickered and kissed Jake again, this time on the lips. Maybe it lasted longer than it should.

Jake yelped and broke the kiss as he received a hail of cashews. He turned indignantly on the team. "What the hell was that for?"

"You can kiss him anytime," Del said. "Put your barman down and pay us some attention."

Jake pouted, laughed and waved at Moose behind the bar. "Beers all round, Moose. On the house."

Cheers erupted around the room as Moose saluted. "Coming up, boss."

Conversation didn't flag all night, with the team's stories getting more outrageous and Howie's eyes getting wider. Jake was pleasantly buzzed when the door opened, letting in the cold night air. He didn't bother to look to see who had come in, but he felt Mitch stiffen.

Jake frowned up at him. "What's the matter?"

Mitch didn't stop staring at the man who walked to the

bar. "I know him."

"Him?" Jake followed his gaze. "Where from?"

Mitch shook his head. "I don't know."

Jake studied the man as he leaned over the bar to talk to Moose. He was dressed in jeans and a well-worn jacket, his boots were similarly used but polished. Possibly ex-military? Moose pointed and when the man turned around, Mitch dug his fingers into Jake's hip.

"Mitch? Do you know him?" Jake asked.

Mitch nodded slowly. "He's my brother."

THE END

ABOUT THE AUTHOR

Sue Brown is owned by her dogs and two teenagers. When she isn't following their orders, she can be found plotting at her laptop.

Sue discovered M/M romance at the time she woke up to find two men kissing on her favourite television series. The series is long gone but the kissing was tender and Sue had a lightbulb moment.

Since then she has written many stories hoping to recreate that tender moment she saw on screen. Sue has high hopes that one day she will provide a lightbulb moment for someone else.

Come over and talk to Sue at:
Her website: http://www.suebrownstories.com/
Facebook: http://www.facebook.com/suebrownstories
Twitter: http://twitter.com/#!/suebrownstories
Email: sue@suebrownstories.com

Available from **Dreamspinner Press:**

Some books available in audio and translations

Nothing Ever Happens

Final Admission

The Layered Mask

Waiting

Made for Aaron in Gothika #1

Falling for Ramos

The Next Call

Stolen Dreams

Chance to be King

The Sky is Dead

The Night Porter Series

The Night Porter

Light of Day

Morning Report Series

Morning Report

Complete Faith

Papa's Boy

Luke's Present

Letters From a Cowboy

Isle Series

The Isle of... Where?

Isle of Wishes

Isle of Waves

Isle of Waiting (in Grand Adventures)

Island Doctor

Island Counselor

Available from **Totally Bound:**
Tumbling Blindly (The Arches #1)
Holding Together (The Arches #2)
Turning Over (The Arches #3)

Available from **Sue Brown Stories:**
Ducks in a Row (in Turning the Page)
Morning My Angel
A Tale Told in Darkness (A Tale Told in Darkness #1)
Close Your Eyes (in Valentine Delights)
Louis Hates Valentine's Day
Racing Raindrops
Mr Plum
Summer's Dawn
Summer's Song
A Cock in the Window

J.T's Bar
Alpha Barman
Alpha Chef (coming May 2017)
Alpha Trucker (coming November 2017)

Angel Enterprises
Morning My Angel
Goodnight My Angel
Angel Enterprises #3 (coming September 2017)

Lyon Road Vets
Hairy Harry's Car Seat
Bob, Destroyer of Leads
Hazel Takes Over
Stormin' Norman

Wolves of Sapphire Ranch
(to be republished 2017)
The Last Wolf
The Hidden Wolf
The Rogue Wolf

With A Kick (with Clare London)
Hissed as a Newt
Bells and Balls

Left at the Crossroads (with Lisa Worrall)
In-Decision

The Fitzwarren Inheritance
(with RJ Scott and Chris Quinton)
The Lord's Tale

70850777R00114

Made in the USA
Columbia, SC
16 May 2017